Pas de deux . . . with the Killmaster!!

Slowly he was losing his grip on Slade's gun hand. At the same time, he realized that the little man was maneuvering him toward the French doors and the balcony.

Carter tried to exert force in the opposite direction, but his strength had ebbed until they were about equal.

Slade maneuvered him closer and closer. Suddenly Carter lunged forward, pulling Slade off-balance. He thrust the man's hand through the shattered pane and raked it from side to side over the jagged glass.

Slade startled, bellowed in pain. As he tried to yank his arm free, Carter put all his weight on it, slashing the arm from elbow to wrist.

Again Slade screamed, this time as much from the fountain of his own blood spewing as from pain. His fingers opened and the gun fell to the deck of the balcony.

NICK CARTER IS IT!

"Nick Carter out-Bonds James Bond."
—*Buffalo Evening News*

"Nick Carter is America's #1 espionage agent."
—*Variety*

"Nick Carter is razor-sharp suspense."
—*King Features*

"Nick Carter has attracted an army of addicted readers...the books are fast, have plenty of action and just the right degree of sex...Nick Carter is the American James Bond, suave, sophisticated, a killer with both the ladies and the enemy."
—*The New York Times*

FROM THE NICK CARTER
KILLMASTER SERIES

BLOODTRAIL TO MECCA

KILL MASTER

NICK CARTER

JOVE BOOKS, NEW YORK

Dedicated to the men of the
Secret Services of the
United States of America

BLOODTRAIL TO MECCA

A Jove Book / published by arrangement with
The Condé Nast Publications, Inc.

PRINTING HISTORY
Jove edition / March 1988

ISBN: 0-515-09490-0

Jove Books are published by The Berkley Publishing Group,
200 Madison Avenue, New York, New York 10016.
The name "JOVE" and the "J" logo
are trademarks belonging to Jove Publications, Inc.

PRINTED IN THE UNITED STATES OF AMERICA

10 9 8 7 6 5 4 3 2 1

ONE

Rachel Zail stepped from the warm night through the beaded curtains into the hot, smoky air of the bar. There were only a few fishermen at this late hour, but as one their heads turned to stare.

The stares made her smile. She was used to men staring at her, and she loved it.

Rachel was young—only nineteen—and tall, and beautiful. Her hair was glossy black and hung like an ebony veil to her shoulders. Her nose and chin were a shade too large, her mouth a shade too wide, and her dark eyes were enormous.

But because of her imposing stature, no one ever noticed that she wasn't a perfect beauty. Her body matched her height, with thrusting breasts and wide hips supported by long, tanned legs.

"*Buenos noches, muchachos*. My friend and I have come to raise a little hell in your establishment. Do you mind?"

There was general laughter from the bartender through the fishermen to a few gypsies at a rear table. The young girl who had been lightly strumming flamenco music on a guitar took it up again. That was a signal for glasses to clink

1

and conversation to continue.

A tall, darkly handsome man with curly black hair and an athlete's physique stepped from the shadows behind Rachel and took her arm.

"Are you sure, Rachel, that you want more to drink? You've already had—"

"Of course I'm sure," she said with a laugh, looping her arm through his and dragging him toward a table. "Wine, señor! Bring us a bottle of your best!"

"In this place," the man whispered, "it's probably colored seawater."

"Shhh, Nollo, mind your manners. These people are simple . . . they just want to have fun."

Her speech was slurred and she weaved a bit in her chair, but no one cared. She was just a young, beautiful girl out with her handsome boyfriend for a night of fun.

The wine came and the man paid, adding a modest tip.

"Do you know something?" she murmured.

"What?" he replied, pouring the wine.

"I let you pick me up . . . let's see, ten hours ago, in Granada, at a party . . ."

"Oh? I thought you picked me up," he teased, grinning.

"No matter," she said, waving one hand. "And now we're in . . . where are we in?"

"Castell de Ferro."

"Yes, Castell de whatever, and I don't even know your last name."

He leaned forward and brushed her bare shoulder with his lips. "Does it matter?"

"Not really. It was a very dull intellectual party with a lot of boring children . . ."

"I thought they were your fellow students."

"They are, and they are boring. Almost as boring as the school."

"Then why do you stay?"

"Because my brother makes me. He wants me to be a great artist, and a year at the academy in the Alhambra will set me on my way. Those are his very words."

"You are very beautiful, Rachel."

"And you are very handsome, Nollo. Would you like to make love to me?"

He chuckled and ran a fingertip down the firm line of her jaw. "You are a wild and impetuous child."

"My brother says that too. But you're both wrong. I'm a wild and impetuous *woman*. You haven't answered my question. Would you like to make love to me?"

"What man wouldn't?"

"Good. Then we will . . . later."

She refilled her glass and clapped her hands in time with the rhythmic beat of the girl's guitar. Rachel Zail was a girl who threw herself into fun the way a diver throws himself from the high board into the water.

Her eyes were alive and her wide mouth was parted in a gleaming smile as she clapped softly, and then louder as the driving beat of the guitar invaded her body.

Suddenly she was on her feet dancing, her body straight, just her hips and feet moving. Then two of the younger men moved out of the shadows in the rear and joined her. As one, they did slow, provocative steps around her.

One of them handed her a pair of castanets, and she used them skillfully. She danced faster, the men danced faster, and the guitar kept pace.

Everyone was clapping now and smiling at her, even the gypsy women who had lost their men to this youthful vixen.

Then it was over and one of the women shouted, *"Olé! Olé! Gitana brava!"*

Rachel fell back into her chair and reached for her glass of wine.

"You dance very well."

"Of course," she shrugged. "I've been dancing the hora since I could walk. Let's have another bottle of wine."

Nollo looked at his watch. "I have a better idea. Let's get a bottle of wine and go down to the beach . . . perhaps a swim?"

Her full lips parted in a wide smile. "Nollo, you are a genius."

Moments later they were walking arm in arm from the bar down the beach to a secluded cove. She moved unsteadily, and now and then pressed the side of a full breast against his arm.

The cove was almost entirely surrounded by rocks, a deep pool with a tiny sand beach. It was deserted, as Nollo knew it would be. There was no road leading to it, and the outlet to the sea was too narrow for anything larger than a small boat.

As they approached the beach, Nollo took a small, fat bottle from his pocket.

He was just reaching into the other pocket for the gauze pad, when Rachel suddenly bolted. She ran like a deer across the sand. At the water's edge, she turned.

"Swimming was a wonderful idea!" she said with a laugh.

Her dress fell to the sand and her hands went to her bra. When she unhooked the front fastening, her heavy breasts burst free in the moonlight. The scant panties were discarded, revealing the triangle of thick dark hair between her slender, supple thighs.

"Well?" she chided. "A swim was your idea. Are you going to do it with your clothes on?"

She turned and waded into the surf, moonlight glinting off her healthy, olive-hued body. The water slowly lapped up the long legs to dampen the hair at her groin. Then she dived forward and rolled to her back.

"Come on! I'll race you to the point and back!" she called, and rolled over into a slow crawl.

Then she was skimming across the water.

"Bitch," Nollo hissed, looking quickly around the beach and to the cliffs of the cove to make sure no one was there.

He hadn't counted on this. But there was nothing he could do. He would have to humor her.

Quickly, he removed his clothes and made a small bundle of them, putting the gauze and the bottle in the center. Then he dived into the water and struck out after her.

Rachel was a good swimmer and she had a head start. She was pleased to see when she looked behind her that he was catching up. With that fantastic body, those powerful arms and legs, he was bound to be a good swimmer.

She smiled to herself. The wine and the warm water had put a rush of fire in her body. Already she was visualizing the mutual seduction that would cap the evening. It wasn't the first time she had made love to a man she had met only hours before.

With that thought, an image of her brother Isser's stern face appeared before her.

She blinked and swam on.

Halfway to the mouth of the cove, she paused. He was right behind her.

"Enough," she said, as he glided forward until their bodies were nearly touching.

"Enough what?"

"Enough swimming," she murmured, sliding her arms around his neck and pressing her breasts to his chest. She extended her tongue and ran it along his lips. "Now we make love."

"Here?" he chuckled.

"Of course not here, silly. We'd probably drown. Back

on the beach!'' She tucked, placed her feet flat on his bare chest, and pushed off. He was right behind her.

I hope, Rachel thought to herself, *that he does everything as well as he swims!*

She came out of the water running. When her feet hit soft, still-warm sand, she sprawled and rolled to her back with her eyes closed.

She heard his feet pad across the sand, pause, and continue. Then she sensed him drop to the sand beside her. She could almost feel his eyes devour her body.

Then he was against her, his touch flooding her body with fire. He drew her into his arms, and Rachel groaned at the sensation of his lips at her nipples.

''Your hands, Nollo, use your hands.''

''Soon.''

His lips found hers and the kiss was electric. She pulled him closer, demanding more. Then his hands were moving up her body, over her breasts, to her throat. The thick hair on his chest tantalized her nipples. She felt the hardness of his body press over hers, and lifted herself to meet him.

Desire welled within her.

Suddenly a wet, evil-smelling cloth was over her mouth and nose. She struggled, the fumes gagging her . . . .

She couldn't breathe. She was choking. She tore at his hands and arms, her nails gouging . . . .

She felt herself growing faint.

And that was all she knew.

He waited until the struggles ended and she was breathing evenly before he lifted the gauze. Then he darted to his clothing and fumbled until he found a small penlight. He directed it out to sea and flashed it three times.

The light had barely faded before there was the sound of a powerful motor launch in the distance.

By the time it had nosed up onto the sand, he was dressed.

Two men jumped from the launch and ran toward them.

"What took so long?"

"The bitch had to frolic in the water."

"By Allah, she is naked!"

"Get her in the boat. We'll put her dress back on there."

Gingerly, the two carried the woman to the boat. Nollo followed, and in minutes they were skimming across the water straight out to sea.

TWO

The big Mercedes dropped out of the Negev, and the myriad lights of Eilat sparkled through the windshield. Isser Zail put his foot to the floor and the speedometer needle climbed steadily.

The car was one of the few luxuries Isser allowed himself, and, like most Israelis, he loved to drive it fast. But that night he had pushed the car to its limit on the treacherous, 140-mile-long road from Beersheba to Eilat for a reason other than that of the sheer joy of speed.

The envelope had been waiting for him in his apartment. It had been slipped under his door. Like a fool, he hadn't opened it at once.

It had been a hard day in the air, tense, up and down the Sinai line. He wanted a shower and a drink. It was nearly seven when he slit it open.

There were four photos—all of his sister Rachel—and a note and a cassette tape. The note was addressed to him, and across the top, in block letters, was a direction to play the tape first.

He heard Rachel's voice:

"Isser, they have kidnapped me. I don't know who they

are or what they want, and I don't know where I am. They have told me to tell you that I am not harmed. I'm not. But I will be if you do not meet their demands—''

The tape abruptly ended, and Isser Zail picked up the note with shaking fingers. It was brief and to the point in carefully scripted, perfect Hebrew:

Major Zail, in Eilat, on the Jordanian side of the Blue Sky Caravan Village, there are several bars along the beach. One of them is called Pippos. Ten tonight. Wear civilian clothes.

"Son of a bitch!" Zail cried out in English, and dived for the phone.

He dialed Rachel's apartment in Granada and let it ring several times. No answer.

Quickly, he thumbed through his address book until he found the name of Louise Bronson, an English girl who was quite friendly with Rachel.

She answered on the second ring.

"Louise, this is Isser Zail, Rachel's brother."

"Oh, yes, hello. Are you in Granada?"

"No. No, I'm home, in Israel. Louise, is Rachel there?"

"No, as a matter of fact I haven't seen her since a party the day before yesterday."

Zail felt a choke grow in his throat. "You mean, she hasn't been in her classes?"

"No . . . but . . ." There was a long pause with something like a sigh at the other end.

"What is it, Louise?"

"Well, Isser, you know Rachel. She sometimes does this, just pops off with someone."

"Is that what happened the day before yesterday?"

"She met him at the party. He was a tall, handsome chap—looked Italian."

"Do you happen to know where they were going?"

"Haven't the faintest. Anything wrong, Isser?"

"No, no, nothing. Thank you, Louise."

Isser Zail dressed quickly in jeans, a T-shirt, and a light leather jacket. He tucked his standard-issue Beretta into his belt and ran for his car.

Now he hit Hatmarim Boulevard and slowed as he moved through the city. In the swankier North Beach area he sped up and cut back to the lagoon leading into the Red Sea. The water lay crystal clear in the moonlight.

He passed the huge caravan park and pulled off to the side on a bluff overlooking the lower beach road. Across the bay, less than a mile away, he could see the twinkling lights of the Jordanian port city of Aqaba. Just to the south was the frontier of Saudi Arabia. Behind him, to the west, were the desolate mountains of the Sinai.

Zail cursed them under his breath. It was obvious why they had chosen this spot to meet him.

He locked the car and walked down the bluff. At the walkway above the lagoon he turned left, and wondered as he approached the lighted buildings if someone were watching him.

Most likely.

The Beretta felt very reassuring beneath his jacket. But what could he do with it without harming Rachel?

His little sister, as wild and tempestuous as she was, was all he had in the world. For as long as he could remember, he had been married to the air force. Rachel, and the promise he had made to his parents to care for her, had become his only life outside the military.

He kept walking at exactly the same pace, not looking around, not turning his head from side to side. His pulse was racing and it seemed suddenly so hot he could hardly breathe.

The little seaside bars were all the same, two-story affairs

with the upper floor an apartment for the owner. There were
five of them. Pippos was the last on the line.

Inside it was dim, and unlike the other bars he had passed,
which blared rock-and-roll, the music here was subdued and
came from a speaker in the rear. The room was a few steps
below the level of the street. It was comfortably gloomy,
with burlap on the walls and indirect lighting. It was filled
with tables having wooden tops scrubbed to a soft, bleached
whiteness, and round-backed chairs.

Frying fish and perfume fought the odor of beer as Zail
let his eyes wander over the crowd. It was mostly young,
sprinkled with a few middle-aged tourists in couples.

Zail didn't know who he was looking for, but none of
this crowd filled the bill he anticipated.

He moved toward the rear where it was less crowded.
Several tables away was a buxom girl with flaming red hair.
She was wearing a blue waitress uniform. She leaned forward over the table while a grimy, unshaven man whispered
in her ear. Suddenly she threw her head back and laughed
raucously.

In so doing, she saw Zail and stood. She said something
to the man. He nodded and patted her rear as she walked
to Zail's table.

"Beer?"

He nodded. "A large bottle."

Again he looked around. His eye fell on a pretty dark-
haired teen-ager sitting by herself near the bar. She was
dressed in the traditional uniform:—cut-off jeans, a T-shirt
over braless breasts, and sandals. Her hair was like a black
curly cap on her head.

She smiled, and Zail looked away. He checked his watch.
He was twenty minutes late.

Damn, he thought, *surely they wouldn't leave*.

"Two hundred," the waitress said, setting a glass and bottle in front of him.

He dropped two bills on the table and she returned to her friend.

Zail drank and waited. People left and more came. Only once in the next hour did anyone enter who looked the part.

He was about thirty, sloppily dressed in a dark sweater, with glossy black hair that grew low on his forehead. His complexion was pasty and his nose was beaked.

As he drank a beer at the bar, his eyes met Zail's. They were dead, as though he might have enjoyed pulling the wings from flies as a child. And probably still enjoyed it.

Zail tensed, but the man looked away and left soon after.

"Hello."

It was the lone teen-ager with the black mop-top. He hadn't seen her approach the table from the side. Now she had an enormous bag slung from her shoulder.

Isser Zail nodded. "Hello."

"Buy a girl a drink?" Her Hebrew was perfect without a hint of an accent.

"Sorry, I'm waiting for someone."

"Oh, come now, Major, don't be a tightwad."

As she slid into the chair opposite him, she removed her earrings and slid them across the table.

He recognized them immediately, and looked up. This close, she didn't look so young. There were tiny lines around her eyes, and the eyes themselves had many miles in them.

"You?"

"Me, Major. Give me a cigarette and look as if you're enjoying my company."

Transfixed by her gall, Zail shook a cigarette from his pack. She took it, wet it with the tip of her tongue, and put it in her mouth. Zail held his lighter in both hands to keep it steady.

"Who the hell are you?"

"That's not important," she said, taking the cigarette from her mouth and exhaling so the smoke wreathed around his head.

"All right, then, what bunch of fanatics do you represent?"

She ran her tongue over her lips and smiled. The smile was like a cat's, perfectly turned up at the corners. "The homeless people of our world, all those you have stolen from. Sit down! . . . and smile. You wouldn't want anyone to get the idea we're not getting along, would you?"

Zail eased back into his chair. Indeed, this was no teenager. Her voice and now her face were as hard as nails. "What do you want? I have very little money."

"We have more money than we'll ever spend."

"What, then?"

"You're on two-on, two-off flight schedules at the Beersheba air base, are you not?"

"Yes."

"Testing the new fighter-bombers the Zionists have just purchased from America?"

Zail's eyes narrowed. "How do you know so much?"

"We know. We will go now for a romantic walk along the beach."

"Go to hell."

"Major Zail, you will do exactly as I say and listen very closely to what I tell you, or tomorrow and every day thereafter for as long as it takes, you will receive a package. In those packages will be pieces of your sister. Shall we walk now?"

Moving through the bar, she slid her arm through his. It was all Isser Zail could to to keep his hands off her throat.

Outside, she left the board walkway and moved down to the beach. Here she walked until they were in total darkness hidden among the dunes. Zail followed her, his hand now and then moving back and forth over the Beretta even though he knew he wouldn't use it.

"This is good here." She dropped to the sand and began rummaging in her bag. "Sit."

"Where is my sister, you bitch?"

"She is in the desert. She is well, and for the time being she is well cared for. Sit!"

He dropped beside her. "What do you want?"

"A plane."

"You're mad."

"The whole world is mad, Major Zail." She spread a topography map out on the ground and began playing the shaft of a penlight over it. "Three days from now, you again have the duty. You also have night flights this time. You leave the air base at Beersheba at midnight. In a three-plane formation you fly north—"

"How in God's name do you know all of this?"

"Do you think only your precious Mossad has an intelligence system, Major? Now, shut up and listen. Here, at the Dead Sea, the formation breaks for solo reconnaissance. One plane will return over Jordan. The other will make a pass over southern Lebanon. You move west over Zefat and the ocean."

Isser Zail jumped to his feet. "I won't listen to this nonsense any longer!"

She began folding the map. "Very well. You'll get the first package tomorrow. Shall we say, an ear?"

Zail grabbed her by the throat. He brought her to her feet and then lifted her a foot from the ground.

"What if I keep you and send *your* ears to them!"

"Don't be naïve, Major. I am dispensible to them. Is your sister dispensible to you?"

He dropped her and sank to his knees himself. "You're

animals! I am a sabra—I was born in Israel!"

"So was I. But we call it Palestine."

"I can't betray my country."

"Very well. The Jordanian frontier is there, ten minutes at a fast jog. Should I go?"

Zail dropped his head into his hands. She took his silence as a go-ahead, and unfolded the map.

"You will begin sending a Mayday here, just south of Cyprus as you start your southern leg toward the Sinai. Here, at thirty-three degrees longitude and thirty-four degrees latitude, you will descend to three hundred feet. At approximately thirty-two point eight degrees latitude, or roughly one hundred miles from land, you will see a towed plane. Never mind what kind. It will leave the proper debris when it is blown up . . ."

"My God, do you think something this insane can be pulled off?"

She ignored him. "You will drop your spare tanks and kill your radio at the point of explosion. This is for your own good, so you can return to Israel."

"You are mad! You think I can deliver a three-million-dollar airplane to our enemies and my country will never know I did it?"

"Your people, Major, will think that you crashed in the Mediterranean. Still at three hundred feet or less, you will turn east. You will enter Libya here, thirty miles west of Tobruk. Fly due south. Fifty miles into the desert south of Abyar al Hakim, you will see a runway marked with lights."

She folded the map and laid it in the sand between them. Then she lit a cigarette, stood, and walked down to the water. For five minutes she stood near the water, smoking. Only once did she look back at the kneeling figure. At the end of that time, she went back and knelt beside him.

"Your sister will be smuggled to Cyprus by boat. From

there she will be flown back to Spain. You will be dropped, with the raft from your plane, off the coast near Port Said.''

He looked up at her, but he didn't speak. She took the map and slipped it into the side pocket of his jacket.

''You have twenty-four hours, Major Zail. We'll be in touch.''

He watched her jog down the beach and around the point that led to the frontier. Only when she was out of sight did he begin to weep

Major Isser Zail lay across the bed in only his shorts. His body was lathered with perspiration and the room reeked of gin and stale tobacco.

He had driven back from Eilat at a snail's pace, arriving just before dawn. In his apartment, he had undressed, opened the bottle, and spread out.

Other than refilling his glass, he hadn't moved since. Now half of a second bottle was empty and the lights of Beersheba twinkled outside his window.

He tried to read his watch, but the hands seemed to swim in front of his eyes.

He had noticed the need to visit the bathroom an hour before, but could not make his muscles work. Now he knew he would have to make the trip or bathe himself in his own waste.

He had just struggled to his feet when the telephone rang.

''Yes?''

''Major Zail?'' A man's voice. English, heavily accented.

''Yes.''

''Isser? Oh, God, Isser, is it you?''

''Rachel! Rachel, are you all right?''

She was sobbing. ''Isser, I don't know what's happening! I'm afraid. What do they want from us?''

''Rachel, have they hurt you?''

"They hit me once, but I'm all right. But they—'' She blubbered again. "Isser, they said they were going to cut off my ears!'' Suddenly her voice rose, near hysteria. "My ears, for God's sake! They're going to cut off my ears—''

There was a scream and her voice was cut off, to be replaced by the man's.

"Major Zail . . .''

"You son of a cheap whore . . .''

"What is your decision, Major? I have no time for idle name-calling.''

Now Isser Zail was cold sober. The sweat on his body had suddenly turned cold, forming an icy chill deep in his gut.

"Major Zail, are you still there?''

"I'm here.''

"It is your move, Major.''

"I'll do it, you bastards.''

"A wise decision, Major. We will await you.''

The line went dead, and something in Isser Zail died with it.

THREE

There was a heavy afternoon mist on the river as the cab passed over the Vauxhall Bridge to the south bank of the Thames. When it reached Kennington Oval, Nick Carter leaned forward from the rear seat.

"This will be fine."

"Right you are, mate." The cabbie pulled to the side and flipped the flag. "That'll be five pound ten."

Carter gave him a ten and stepped from the cab. Away from the river, the fog wasn't so heavy.

He started through the small park. Unkempt grass littered with paper wound through the trees.

St. James's it isn't, Carter thought, rounding the corner of a monument. He practically ran into a pair of lovers. The girl was half perched on a low ledge, her skirt to her hips. Her boyfriend was working studiously between her spread legs.

" 'Ere now, who you spyin' on, mate?" The girl's feet hit the ground and the boy hastily zipped up.

"Excuse me," Carter said, moving around them.

"You must not 'a heard me, friend."

The boy was big, inches taller than Carter and as broad

through the shoulders. The hand on Carter's shoulder was like a slab of beef with fingers.

"I said excuse me."

"S'okay, Jamey, let 'im go."

"Let 'im go me arse . . ."

"Take your hand off my shoulder." The voice was calm, a monotone.

"Put me 'and through yer face, that's what I'll do . . ."

Carter was in a hurry and he didn't want to hurt the boy. If it came to bare hands, he would have to.

"Why don't you just get back to your girl friend and I'll be on my way."

The boy swung.

Carter sidestepped easily.

When the young man turned for another swing, he was looking cross-eyed into the muzzle of a 9mm Luger.

"Jamey, 'e's got a gun!"

"B'gawd, don't ya think I can see that?"

"Good-bye, son," Carter whispered. "Run, that way, until you're out of breath."

Together the boy and girl took off across the grass.

Carter continued on out of the park. He crossed the oval into a narrow street bordered with trees. The trees looked tired, their boles scarred with pierced hearts, initials, and various emblems of local gangs.

Mayfair it isn't, Carter thought, turning off into an even narrower street.

A red setter, lying square in the middle of the street, lifted his head as Carter passed, then let it fall with a thud.

Twice Carter stopped in the shelter of a tree, peering behind him. The setter lay still, the only living thing between Carter and the swirling fog at the end of the street.

Then he spotted the number he wanted. He pushed open a white, barred gate, and walked up a driveway lined with poplars. Off to the left, a sleek, late-model Rolls sat in a cobbled courtyard under a canopy.

The house was mock Tudor, with an arched doorway and two bells. He rang both. A moment later he heard the thud of heels on a wooden floor and the door opened.

It was a housekeeper, short, dark, with a pinched face and a squat body stuffed into a black dress and overflowing a white apron tied around her waist.

"Yes?"

"I'd like to see Mr. Parnoque."

"Yes?"

"I'm expected. I'm the man from Washington."

"Come in."

Carter stepped inside a dark hall that smelled of flowers.

"This way."

As Carter followed her down the hall, he felt a jolt of anticipation feed adrenaline into his body.

Two months. For two long months he had tried to find a lead, a way in, a chink in the armor of a mad terrorist group called the Sons of Islam. He and other agents had put the word out all over Europe, Africa, and the Middle East. For weeks, nothing.

But now, maybe something.

They came to a pair of massive doors. A suit of armor and helmet stood improbable sentry beside them.

A growl answered her knock and she moved inside, with Carter behind her.

"The man from Washington, sir."

Oliver Parnoque hoisted his 350-pound bulk from an easy chair and approached. He waved one fat finger at the housekeeper and followed her out the door with dark, button eyes.

When the door closed behind her, he lifted his hand. "Nick."

"Oliver. It was good hearing from you, believe me."

Parnoque laughed in reply. It was more like a wheeze. "You should have come to me in the first place. Everyone else does."

"My agency can't always afford your prices."

The big man shrugged. "More legwork for you when they can't. Come, sit. We'll both sit, here by the fire. I think better sitting on my large derriere, afflicted as I am with our great Henry's disease, fat."

They sat and Carter was offered a cigar. He shook his head and lit a cigarette.

"Those will kill you," Parnoque growled.

"So will your fat."

Another wheeze. "Too true, too true. I don't suppose you want sherry?"

Carter made a face, and a bottle of good scotch appeared.

"Three fingers, one cube. There you are."

Carter took his glass, touched the other man's, and drank. "Nice neighborhood."

"No different than the area around my other domiciles around the world. It reminds me of my urchin roots."

How true that is, Carter thought. He had visited many of them on just such a mission as this one.

Oliver Parnoque had homes in Geneva, Berlin, Paris, Madrid, Hong Kong, and God-only-knew where else. And in each place, he had eyes and ears.

The man was a fixer, a go-between, a liaison between any two or more parties trying to get together. He was a mediator and an intelligence gatherer. He was also a buyer and seller of information, the very best information.

"Well?" Carter asked.

The man settled plump hands on his stomach. "Ah, you Yanks, never enough time, always in a hurry. The folder there, on the table in front of you."

Carter opened the folder. It contained two eight-by-ten

glossy color photographs and four neatly typed sheets of paper.

Both photographs were of the same woman. The first one Carter looked over was full length on a beach, in profile. Her tall, lithe body was tanned a deep gold, and a mass of blond hair, bleached nearly white from the sun, floated about her shoulders. She wore a scrap of bright red bikini, and gold chains, one around her neck and the other encircling her waist.

The chains did almost as much as the bikini in containing or disguising the ample abundance of very voluptuous curves.

The second picture was a frontal head and shoulders shot.

It was more than just a beautiful face. It didn't matter that her mouth was slightly too broad for the delicate, heart-shaped face. Or that the fine, straight nose stopped just short of classic elegance. Her eyes were a marvel—large, thickly lashed, with a slight tilt at the corners. They were the deepest green Carter had ever seen.

But they weren't there. That was her flaw. The eyes were vacant. It was as if they saw, but didn't transmit to the brain what they were seeing.

"Her name is Constance Graves. She's British, a London model and part-time actress. She made quite a sensation a few years ago doing a totally nude dance in some West End musical."

Carter looked up. "Why am I interested in her?"

"Because, Nick, for the last two years she has been the mistress of Marcel Isban."

Carter's whole body tensed and a smile, almost evil, parted his lips.

Marcel Isban held the purse strings of one of the largest of the Middle Eastern fanatical terrorist groups: the Sons of Islam. Agencies all over the world knew who Isban was and what he did, but they couldn't pin him down.

For years the Sons of Islam—even though they were strong in numbers—had been semidormant. Then, about a year before, they had suddenly had a tremendous infusion of cash. Almost at once they had jumped back into the fray with kidnappings, bombings, hijackings, and the formation of new cells.

Two months ago they had become so open and so notorious that the problem had been dumped in the lap of AXE, the U.S. government's supersecret intelligence arm that specialized in termination.

And AXE's top terminator was Nick Carter, designation N3, Killmaster.

Parnoque continued. "As I'm sure you know, Marcel Isban is a satyr. His lust for female flesh is equalled only by his hatred for Israel."

"And this Constance Graves satisfies that?"

"Evidently more than any other woman he had ever known. They met in London, and after tasting the lady's charms for only one night, Isban carted her off to his villa in Algiers. The top page there will give you a rundown on the lady's sexual adventures. Apparently she is quite insatiable."

Carter scanned the page and whistled. "Some of this happened while she was with Isban."

"Quite so," Parnoque said, nodding. "He doesn't seem to mind a bit as long as she relates it all to him in the minutest detail."

"Don't tell me, Oliver, that she is your client?"

"Ah, Nick, but she is. It just so happens that her offer to *sell* certain information came to me about the time I received your query to *buy* certain information."

"She took off on Isban?"

"It would appear so. The lady evidently got bored in

Algiers. She has a history of that.''

Again Carter picked up the head shot. "Her eyes," he said. "She looks doped in this picture."

The huge man chuckled. "I thought you would catch that. It's not the case."

"What, then?"

"Believe it or not, Nick, with all of her beauty and her randy desire, the woman is the prototype of the dumb blonde. What you see in those eyes is vacant stupidity. Other than her constant search for sexual conquest, and her equal lust for money, the woman has not had an intelligent thought in her head her entire life."

Carter shook his head, already wondering if this visit was a total loss. "I take it she's running?"

"Yes. The other three pages are transcripts of our conversations. I think there is enough there, plus what she hasn't told me, so that you will be interested."

Carter perused the pages. "If she does have all this, I could use it."

"I thought so."

"How much does she want?"

"Come, come, Nick, the fee I charge only covers putting the two of you together. Whatever deal you make with this beautiful airhead is up to you."

Carter hitched his chair closer to Parnoque and leaned forward. "All right, it's worth the gamble. Where do I find her?"

"Constance Graves has already paid me *her* half of my usual fee," Pernoque answered with a thick-lipped, lopsided grin.

Carter took an envelope from his inside pocket and placed it in the fat man's lap. In it was ten thousand dollars.

Oliver Parnoque didn't work cheap.

But then, Carter thought, his overhead probably matched

the budget of several Third World countries.

"I gave her several instructions. One of them was to color that mane of hers black or dark brown. There were others. I only hope she follows them."

"Where?" Carter asked softly.

"She is checking into the La Réserve at Beaulieu tomorrow under the name of Wilby, Grace Wilby."

"The Riviera? You think that's wise?"

The fat man shrugged. "Of course not. But the idiot contends that she cannot go three whole days without the sun and her creature comforts."

"All right. How do I meet her?"

"That's up to you. But I suggest you do it outside her suite, initially. A chance pickup would be best, I think— perhaps the beach or the bar."

Carter replaced the papers and photos in the folder. "I can take these?"

"Of course, and this." He dropped a ring in Carter's palm. It was a wide gold band with several good diamonds and two large emerald baguettes. "From one of her many previous admirers, I assume. It's inscribed inside. That will identify you."

Carter pocketed the ring and the folder. "You'll inform her I'm coming?"

"At once." Parnoque heaved his bulk from the chair and extended his hand. "One last piece of information, free."

"I'm listening."

"My ears tell me they have a team looking for you. Evidently, you have gotten close enough in the last month or so."

"I have," Carter said. "But not close enough to give them much of a hard time."

"No matter. You have scratched a few itches they would

rather have left alone. Watch yourself.''

"Do you think they may connect this Graves woman to
me?''

A belly laugh erupted from the big man's lips. "Oh,
Lord, no. Marcel Isban has probably just written the woman
off. He wouldn't want his comrades in the Sons of Islam
to think that his carnal desires had compromised them.''

Carter took his leave and hit the street. The fog had turned
damp now, and as he walked back through the park he
turned his collar up against it.

Back on the main road, he searched vainly for a cab and
settled for a bus. He sat on the upper deck, at the back,
where he could see anyone who got on.

Oliver Parnoque's warning had to be taken seriously. If
the Sons of Islam had put a team after him, Parnoque's
people would know about it.

He rode the bus to South Kensington and took the tube
to Knightsbridge. From there it was a zigzagging, twelve-
block walk to the small, out-of-the-way hotel.

None of it did any good. He spotted them as he mounted
the steps leading into the hotel. There was one on the corner,
one in the driver's seat of a Toyota, probably rented, and
one sitting in the window of a pub across the street.

If there was any doubt, it was erased when he asked for
his key at the desk.

"A gentleman was asking for you, Mr. Coyle. I told him
you were out.''

"Yes, I was expecting him,'' Carter lied. "Thank you.''

Double-locking his room from the inside, he moved to
the window. Two of them were still there. The one in the
Toyota was gone. Ten to one he had gone around to the
alley in the rear to watch the service entrance, Carter figured.

He lit a cigarette and put his mind to work. If Constance

Graves could flesh out the bare bones she had given Oliver
Parnoque, he might have a lever at last. With any luck he
could use her information to track down the cells they had
formed, and locate the source of their sudden wealth.

Now that he had a name and a lead, hours—even minutes—regained importance.

He filled the bathroom sink with cold water and submerged his head. Getting out of England was the problem
now. Like a child, he blew in the water, sending the bubbles
of air exploding around his ears.

He dried himself vigorously. Then, unlocking the door
of his room, he went down to the next floor. The phone
booth there had an outside line. He dialed from memory
and the answer was prompt.

"Amalgamated Press and Wire Services."

"Research, please."

Another pleasant female voice came on the line, and Carter identified himself. Seconds later, the familiar clipped
tones of AXE London's station chief, Jarvis Whitney, came
through.

"Yes, Nick. Trouble?"

"Maybe. I dealt with Parnoque, and I think we have a
live one."

"Good. Are you coming in?"

"No, I've picked up a team. I'll need a little help losing
them, and then a quiet way out of the country, unseen."

"One moment, old chap." He was back in just that time.
"There's a NATO flight to Brussels out of Harcourt in two
hours."

"Fine. You know my location."

"Yes."

"I'll need a vehicle going past in exactly"—he checked
his watch—"twenty minutes."

"How about an ambulance complete with siren?"

"Sounds good."

"Twenty minutes . . . mark."

"Mark," Carter said, and hung up.

He didn't return to his room for his bag. Traveling light and discarding clothing in the field was an occupational hazard in the business.

Through a window in the rear of the second floor, he checked the alley. The watcher was at the open end of the alley. Carter went down the stairs and out the rear door. As he walked toward the end of the alley, he lit a cigarette.

As he passed the man he whirled, flipping the cigarette into his face. When the man's hand automatically came up to shield his eyes, Carter crotch-kicked him.

The howl of pain died when the Killmaster chopped him across the neck on the way down. In seconds, Carter had dragged him behind a row of trash cans and gone through his pockets. Other than some money, cigarettes, and a lighter, he found nothing. But strapped to his right ankle under his pants was a silenced Beretta.

Carter took the gun and reentered the hotel. He walked by the desk, dropping his key, and went on out the front door.

The fog was thick and gauzy now, but he could make out both of them. The drinker had vacated the pub and gone to the Toyota. He was to Carter's left. The other one lolled in the doorway of a millinery shop to his right. It was past five. In this neighborhood, it was a good bet the shop was closed.

Carter turned to his right. Halfway there, he darted into a liquor store. He bought a bottle of cheap wine and came back out.

The Toyota was staying put.

Carter slipped the bottle of wine inside his jacket, and

his hand, holding the Beretta, into the paper bag.

At the millinery shop doorway, he halted abruptly and stepped in. The man was already pulling his hand from under his coat. Carter grabbed the wrist with his left hand and brought up the bag.

Carter shot him twice in the chest and let him slide down the glass door. He opened the wine, poured a third of the liquid over the man's shoulders, and shoved the bottle in his lap between his legs.

Then he crouched beside the dead man and checked his watch.

Four minutes to go.

He waited two minutes, then headed back toward the Toyota. He was still twenty feet from the car when he saw the man's open-mouthed look of shock.

Number One hadn't emerged from the alley. Number Two was still in the doorway.

The question was in this one's eyes: *What the hell am I supposed to do?*

Then he heard the siren, and a second later the orange and white vehicle rounded the corner.

Carter slowed his pace to time it just right. This one he didn't want to kill. He wanted this one to find his friends, clean up the mess, and play messenger boy.

The ambulance and Carter hit the Toyota at precisely the same time. Carter could see the driver and a second man in a white jacket through the windshield.

The second man was Jarvis Whitney himself.

Carter dropped to one knee and flung the bag from the Beretta. Seeing the gun, the man in the Toyota dived. Carter emptied the clip into both driver's-side tires and flung the gun under the car.

Whitney already had the rear doors of the ambulance

open. The Killmaster jumped in and they careened up the
street.

The Toyota's driver had started the car and had come
about half a block before the tires started to leave the rims.

"Any trouble other than that?" Whitney asked.

"Nothing out of the ordinary," Carter replied, lighting
a cigarette.

FOUR

The dark-haired woman who walked into the lobby of La Réserve made every head turn in her wake. Her soft beige dress beneath a chic linen jacket hugged her figure as if it were poured on. Its style was a masterpiece of costly simplicity.

Her skin glowed with a deep golden tan, and when she pulled off the dark glasses, her eyes were such a sparkling green that they made the concierge's hands shake.

"I'm Grace Wilby. I've a suite booked for three nights." Her voice was that of a little girl. That, and the Cockney twang of her speech, raised an eyebrow or two. They didn't fit with the astonishing figure, the cool beauty, and the assured carriage.

"Certainly, mademoiselle. Will you sign here, please?"

She made a study of signing her name, then led a caravan of five bellmen loaded with bags to the elevator.

All the way up in the elevator, the woman's face held an enigmatic smile. Actually, she wanted to shout with glee. She was free at last, and in a few days she would be even more free.

Not that she hadn't enjoyed her fling with Marcel. The

sex was wonderful. The man was like a stallion and constantly ready.

But Algiers? Dear God, the armpit of the earth! And Marcel was gone so much. Not another man in the city would touch her while he was away.

Boring.

The suite was lovely, with richly upholstered white and gilt furniture, elaborately carved headboard and chest, plush carpeting, and bronze and crystal lighting fixtures. And the view of the sea was magnificent.

Maybe she would stay the whole week.

The bellmen scattered her bags through the bedroom and filed out. The bell captain himself, a dark-eyed man of about thirty, with a flashing smile and a body that fairly rippled beneath his uniform, paused to hand her the key.

"Will there be anything else, mademoiselle?"

"Yeah, some champagne, if ya please." She took the key and slipped a fifty-franc note into his hand.

My Gawd, she thought, *he looks like a young Belmondo.* Did she dare? That awful Parnoque man had said, *Be careful who you talk to—no one, if possible—and try to keep a low profile. I think, dear lady, that can be best achieved by keeping your legs crossed.*

The swine!

But surely, a bell captain . . .

"Of course, mademoiselle, right away."

The hell with it, she thought.

"And . . . bring it yerself."

"If you wish."

"I wish."

He left, and she hurried through the bedroom into the bath. The bath was all in pink and gray marble with a huge vanity, a sunken tub, and twin sinks.

She peeled out of the dress and stepped in front of the

mirror. She was completely naked. She never wore underwear.

For a good ten minutes she admired herself in the full-length mirror. It was one of her favorite pastimes.

She heard the door to the sitting room click, and quickly dabbed perfume at her throat and between her breasts. Then, still nude, she ran to the bed.

"Mademoiselle?"

"Yeah, bring it in 'ere!"

He stepped into the room and paused, his eyes taking it all in at one glance.

" 'Ere, beside the bed."

"*Oui, mademoiselle.*" He set the tray down and straightened up, his eyes never leaving the rise and fall of her full breasts. "Will there be anything else?"

"Do you think I 'ave a beautiful body, monseeyure?"

"*Magnifique, mademoiselle,*" he replied.

She rolled to the side of the bed and slowly removed his clothing down to a minuscule pair of briefs.

Then she lay back and let her eyes drink in what she saw.

He was tall, very well built, and he was deeply tanned all over. His muscles bulged as he flexed them for her.

She felt a familiar tingle stir deep inside her.

She loved what she saw. This one had the kind of masculine strength that wrapped around you, and kept on wrapping.

"Yeah," she grinned. "There will be somethin' else."

He smiled as he peeled the briefs down his legs and kicked them away.

Outside, at the end of the hall, a short, heavyset man in a rumpled summer suit sat in a Venetian pearwood chair. His elbows rested on the chair's arm while he supported his rounded double chin on the back of thick, clasped hands.

The weight of his head on the back of his hands squashed his pursed thin lips upward into a petulant look of contempt.

Beneath drooping, half-closed lids, his tar-black eyes darted from the door to a watch on his hairy wrist.

It had been exactly a half hour since the bell captain had entered Constance Grave's suite.

He nodded with satisfaction, rose, and walked to the elevator.

He left the lobby and passed through a courtyard of cascading greenery, neatly bordered grass, and bamboo chairs and tables alive with beautiful people.

Near the pool was a bank of four telephones. He entered the first booth and carefully closed the door behind him. When the proper coins had been dropped, he dialed the number.

"Loew's Monte Carlo," the voice said from seven miles away.

"Four-twenty-six, please."

"*Oui.*"

A few clicks, and a deep, resonant voice answered in English, "Hello?"

The caller replied in staccato Arabic. "She has arrived and already bedded."

A chuckle, and the reply, also in Arabic: "I would expect nothing different. What a silly little thing she is, writing her destination, her hotel, and her assumed name on a pad beside my own phone!"

Now the caller chuckled. "You didn't bring her to Algiers for her brains, Marcel."

"I know," Marcel Isban sighed, "she will be a loss. She has dyed her hair?"

"Yes, just as you guessed from the bottle she left."

"Anything else?"

"No. Is he still there?"

"Yes," Isban replied. "Still gambling below in the casino, and, they tell me, still losing. I'll talk to him later, when the anger of losing is still high in his veins."

"Should I return?"

"Yes, we'll fly out tonight. Oh . . ."

"Yes?"

"Whom did she pick up?"

"The bell captain, right after she arrived."

"How sad. I thought I had improved her taste. *Ciao.*"

"*Ciao*, Marcel."

Ian Slade grunted with disgust and pushed himself from the table. He took the last two chips from what had earlier been a very large pile, dropped them in the croupier's pocket, and headed for the door.

Emerging from the baccarat rooms, he headed for the lounge bar. He was nearly there, threading his way through the tables, when a voice at one of them stopped him.

"Cleaned out, Ian?"

His small wiry body tensed, as it always did when he was caught unawares. Slowly he turned, and then relaxed slightly.

"Hello, Marcel. Traveling the same, beaten paths, I see."

"Don't we all? Sit, I'd like to buy you a drink."

Ian Slade rubbed the fingers of his right hand together. It was a nervous habit that helped him think.

"Sure, why not?"

He slid into a chair opposite the other man and ordered a Campari and soda. Isban ordered Perrier. Slade rarely drank. When he did, it was light. The drink order brought a smile to Isban's lips.

"Still not a drinker, eh?"

"Like you, Marcel, women and the tables are my only vices."

The drinks came, and the two men studied each other over their glasses.

Both were handsome men, somewhere in their forties, with wavy black hair graying slightly at the temples. There, however, the comparison ended.

Marcel Isban was tall, well over six feet, with a superb, well-toned body kept that way by constant exercise. He might have been Greek, with his straight nose and rounded chin. But the eyes were not Greek. Almond-shaped, set slightly aslant under tilted brows, they were a surprising light gray in contrast with his deeply tanned skin.

The eyes and his first name were all his French mother had given Marcel Isban. The rest of him was a pure heritage from his Palestinian father.

Ian Slade, on the other hand, was a foot shorter with a slight body. He had been born and raised in Belfast, and by the time he was twenty he had already killed enough men to match his age.

"It's good to see you, Ian."

"Is it?"

"Of course. It's always good to see old friends."

"Bullshit," Slade said, and lit a small cigar.

"Did the tables wipe you out tonight, Ian?"

"Not quite. I always keep a thousand or so in my sock."

"Good, you know I like a man who thinks ahead. Are you working, Ian?"

"Not at the moment."

"Would you like to be working, Ian?"

Ian Slade averted his eyes and glanced along the bar. Besides the usual crowd, and a few tourists more interested in gawking than gambling, there were three very high-class prostitutes surveying the room.

One, a blonde near the curve of the bar, was five steps above the other two. A black organza-over-silk dress beautifully shaped her full breasts and narrow waist. The neckline was cut in a wide vee that exposed the swell of her breasts and the elegant line of her collarbones. The skirt was parted, revealing the long line of her perfect legs.

Ian Slade sighed and turned back to the other man. He leaned far forward and lowered his voice.

"I don't do your kind of work any more, Marcel."

What Ian Slade meant was that he no longer took on political contracts. He had done two for Marcel Isban, and they had been messy. Both times had been hell getting in and out, and he'd almost been nailed each time.

The money was good, but not if you couldn't live to spend it.

"What if I were to tell you, Ian, that this is personal, not an organization thing?"

Slade rolled his glass in his fingers and looked back at the black dress. Her eyes caught his and she smiled.

"Personal?" he asked.

"Yes. I've had a bit of a problem. Care to discuss it?"

"I'll discuss it."

Isban stood. "Shall we get some air on the promenade?"

The two men moved through the tables and exited to the wide stone promenade that ran the length of the hotel casino above the ocean. Once away from the door, Isban handed Slade a snapshot.

"Very nice."

"Yes, and extremely . . . athletic. But I'm afraid even I am no match for her."

"You said 'personal,' Marcel."

They stopped by the balustrade. Isban seemed to weigh this, and then made a decision, shrugging his wide shoulders in the expensive tuxedo.

"She was my mistress for quite some time. Now she has decided to venture off. Needless to say, I cannot have someone who has been privy to my affairs running around the world, gossiping in a thousand bedrooms.''

''The usual price?''

''This is out of my own pocket, Ian.''

The smaller man smiled, showing crooked teeth. ''It's not entirely personal.''

A chuckle. ''You're so right, you little wretch. Very well, fifteen thousand.''

''And a first-class ticket to . . . let's say, Hong Kong. That's a nice place to cool off for a while.''

''You're a true businessman, Ian. She's registered under the name of Grace Wilby, at La Réserve in Beaulieu, suite Nine hundred. Also, she's a brunette now. She has taken the suite for only three days. Can I count on it being done in that time?''

''I don't see any reason why not.''

''Good, good. Try to make it look like a robbery. She does have quite an interesting array of jewels I'm sure you can get rid of. I'm flying out tonight. Here's a number where you can reach me anytime if there are complications.''

Ian Slade slipped the photo and the piece of paper into his jacket pocket. The two of them headed back toward the French doors.

Suddenly Slade stopped, grasping the other man's elbow. ''Marcel?''

''Yes?''

''Fifteen thousand, the airline ticket to Hong Kong, *and* that black dress at the end of the bar.''

''My dear Ian, you have very expensive tastes.''

''Of course I do, when you're paying.''

Isban laughed. ''Where are you staying?''

''The Balmoral, room Five-twenty-one.''

The bigger man shook his head. ''She will wonder how on earth you can afford her.''

A half hour later, the tall, statuesque blonde in the stunning black dress was picking up her change, ready to call it a night, when a short, fat man in a rumpled suit laid a note in front of her on the bar.

She looked at it: *Hotel Balmoral room 521.*

She looked at him. "You?"

"No, a friend. It's his birthday."

"But, monsieur, the Hotel Balmoral?" she scoffed. "I think you should send your friend to the docks in Nice!"

An envelope joined the note. She thumbed it open and riffled three one-thousand-franc notes.

"My friend will be waiting, mademoiselle."

"I'll wish your friend a very happy birthday, monsieur."

FIVE

By the time Carter completed a commercial flight from Brussels to Paris and caught an early-evening commuter into Nice, it was close to nine.

Emerging from the airport terminal, he toyed with the idea of a hotel and discarded it. Like Oliver Parnoque, the Sons of Islam had eyes and ears everywhere; perhaps not as extensive, but there was always the chance.

Besides, with his day-old beard, rumpled clothes, and no baggage other than the small, gift-wrapped parcel containing his equipment, he wouldn't be welcome in most hotels.

He took his turn at a cabstand and noticed the grimace on the driver's face when he climbed in. "*Le quai.*"

"*Oui, monsieur.*"

It was ten minutes into the city, and another fifteen winding through the heavy summer tourist traffic to the port. The driver was surprised and effusive at the size of the tip.

Carter took a fast turn around the horseshoe-shaped port, and found a restaurant quieter than most. He ordered bouillabaisse, and, when it came, found himself devouring it. After a salad and a cup of coffee, he again hit the quai.

It was late enough now, and they started to come out in droves . . . old, young, short, tall, fat, and thin. In common, they all had one thing to offer: themselves.

On just the west side of the quai from the restaurant to the turn, he was propositioned four times. All of them worked out of a hotel. This he didn't want, and they didn't look too savory anyway.

"*Bonsoir, monsieur*. You are alone this evening?"

She was unusual-looking, with wide cheekbones, short, black bangs, full lips, and a bosom that more than filled a tight jacket. She also had ample hips, sturdy legs, and thick ankles. A pair of sensible flat-heeled shoes covered her feet, making Carter think that her toes were ample as well.

She looked like anything but a working girl.

But it was just that—the way she looked—that made him pause and step into the darkened doorway.

"*Oui, mademoiselle*. I am alone."

"Does monsieur wish some company?"

"Perhaps," Carter replied. "Do you have an apartment?"

"Oh, monsieur, the hotel there. It is not expensive."

"*Non, mademoiselle*. I wish to stay the night, and not in a cheap hotel."

Her dark eyes grew wide. "The night, monsieur? The whole night?"

"*Oui*."

Then her eyes narrowed and she took in his appearance. "I think you joke."

Carter had been toying with a five-hundred-franc bill in his pocket. He pulled it out and held it in front of her eyes. "Apartment?"

She bit her lip, frowned, and then tilted her head. "This way."

Carter trailed within a step of her for six long blocks.

She veered off through the parking lot of a great sprawl of glass and stressed concrete that turned out to be a hospital. Beyond the parking lot they turned right on Rue Lascaris.

All the while, the Killmaster kept an eye on his rear. He was ninety-nine percent sure he'd covered his butt out of Brussels and Paris, but caution was the best insurance for survival.

They turned into what was little more than an alley, and walked another block past small, cheap residential hotels until they came to one called La Maison Solaire. She led him through a narrow hallway with a fraying carpet and built-in fish smells. There was a tiny reception desk, probably from the days when the place was a nightly, transient hotel.

Her apartment was on the third floor. She unlocked the door, and Carter moved past her.

The apartment was small but neat and clean. A single light revealed a sofa in a dark Indian print flanked by a pair of low tables.

Carter gauged the sofa. It wouldn't make the most comfortable bed, but it would do.

"Bedroom?" he asked, pointing to a closed door.

"*Oui*," she replied, nodding hesitantly.

It was simple and cozy, with a bed, a dresser, and two easy chairs. There was a tiny bath just off the room. One window looked down on an alley running behind the building. Carter tried it and found that it opened easily.

"What are you doing?"

"Looking around. Closet?"

"*Oui*."

He checked it. The clothes were similiar to the ones she wore, other than four crisp white uniforms. He pulled the skirt of one of them clear of the others and shot her a quizzical glance.

"I am a nurse at the hospital. The pay is very low." She shrugged. "I have a small son to raise."

"I understand."

"You do?"

"Better than you think," Carter said, heading for the bathroom. "Excuse me a moment."

He used the facilities, and stepped back into the bedroom. She had discarded her clothes and now stood, shyly, at the foot of the bed.

Nude, her figure had a certain innocent appeal that her clothes had hidden. Her breasts were large but stood pertly away from her body. Her hips were too heavy and her skin was a stark white, but even that gave her a quality of vulnerability.

"We will go to bed now?"

"No. Put something on and come back to the living room. We'll talk."

"Talk?" Her eyes were really wide now.

"Yeah, talk. Do you have anything to drink?"

"Some brandy," she babbled, "in the cabinet over the refrigerator."

Carter found the brandy and a couple of glasses. In the living room, he scratched around in a desk until he found a pad and pencil.

When she emerged from the bedroom in a white terry-cloth robe belted tightly around her middle, Carter was sipping brandy and making a list.

"You are a strange man."

"Yeah, I know. Sit."

She sat beside him on the sofa, and unconsciously reached for the second glass of brandy that he had poured.

"Do you work tomorrow?"

"Yes."

"Call in sick. Early in the morning, I want you to go out

and buy me everything on this list.'' He tore off the top sheet on the pad and handed it to her. "Can you read my writing?''

"I think so . . . shorts, shirt, trousers, socks, windbreaker— ''

"The sizes are there at the bottom.''

"I see them. A bathing suit, a beach towel, a beach shirt, and a mini-cassette recorder?''

"That's right. And a couple of mini-tapes.'' He laid some bills on the coffee table. "This should more than cover it.''

She eyed him warily and her voice became very quiet. "Are you a criminal, monsieur? Are you running from the police?''

Carter smiled. "Rest assured I'm not that.''

"What then?''

He lifted her chin with one finger. "I'm a spy on a very secret mission, and the fate of the entire civilized world is in your hands.''

She giggled. "I don't believe that, either.''

"Then don't worry about it. Have you got a blanket?''

"Of course, but what for?''

"Warmth, woman. I'm sleeping here on the couch.''

She stared at him for a long moment. Finally she shook her head and walked into the bedroom, returning with a big down comforter.

"You sleep on the couch?''

"Yes, the couch,'' Carter said, moving around the room and turning off the lights. "Good night . . . uh, what is your name?''

"Nanette.''

"My name is Nick. Good night, Nanette.''

Still shaking her head, she walked into the bedroom and closed the door behind her.

Carter undressed and slipped under the comforter. He slid

both the holster and Luger under the sofa. Hugo, his stiletto, he slid under the cushions within easy reach.

He could have made a call to Constance Graves at La Réserve, but there was always the chance that Marcel Isban—contrary to Parnoque's guess—might be going after her. It would be better to case her first and make sure no one was watching her.

He would do that tomorrow . . . somewhere outside her suite, in case she was being watched.

His eyelids started to droop, when he heard the bedroom door open. She stood there, illuminated in the moonlight for several seconds, still in the robe.

"Something?" Carter asked.

She didn't reply at once. Instead, she moved across the room and knelt by the couch, her face close to his.

"Why do you sleep out here?"

"Because, Nanette, I'm renting your couch and a little help . . . not you."

"But you've more than paid for all three."

He moved up and kissed her gently on the cheek. "Go to bed, Nanette."

"This is not right," she murmured.

Her hands slid up the sides of his face and her lips came down on his. A moan slipped from her throat as she opened her mouth, allowing his tongue to glide between her lips.

As the kiss deepened, her robe parted and Carter could feel the hard pebbles of her nipples grazing his chest. Involuntarily, his fingers came up to comb through her hair.

"You're very tempting," he said.

"Am I?" she whispered. "Oh, that is very flattering. I try to be a temptress, but it is hard when you look as I do. I am not very pretty, am I?"

"A lot prettier than you think."

"Then why do you sleep on the couch?"

"Because I am impotent."

Her hand snaked down over the blanket to the base of his belly. "You lie. I want to make love to you and I want you to make love to me. It has been a long time since I have really wanted to make love to a man."

As she spoke, she tugged at the belt of her robe. It parted completely and her fingers moved lightly over his chest.

Carter couldn't resist the invitation. His fingers moved under the robe and began skimming up and down her back in a sensuously light massage. The flesh came alive to his touch and he felt her shiver.

"You have cruel eyes," she whispered, "but your fingers are so gentle."

He moved his hands around to her heavy breasts and continued to stroke her gently. With a sigh, she leaned forward and Carter pressed his lips to each nipple.

She raked her fingers through his hair as his hands slid down her body. Her thighs parted and she groaned when one hand slipped between them and found her.

Neither of them spoke as Carter caressed and teased erotically. Her eyes closed and her lips parted, and Carter's own eyes feasted on the pleasure and excitement her features expressed. She reached out, wanting to caress him, but for the moment Carter wanted only to watch her growing desire.

She moved closer, her lashes fluttering as he, with playful touches, let his tongue trail down her side to her belly and below. Her breathing came in gasps as his mouth moved sensuously up along her sensitive inner thighs.

His tongue and lips tantalized and teased her, making her flesh ripple. He heard her voice, thick with desire and need, cry out his name. Carter's own need was now out of control.

He swung from the couch, lifted her into his arms, and

carried her into the bedroom.

As rampant as his own desire now was, he paused to look down on her as he laid her gently on the bed.

Her face, eyes partially closed, the tip of her tongue wetting her lips, reflected her yearning. Her breathing was heavy, making her full breasts rise and fall provocatively.

He slid into the bed beside her and she clung to him, hungry for the touch of his naked body against hers.

"Now," she moaned.

"Soon."

Her hands explored his powerful, heavily muscled body. He enjoyed the obvious delight she took in exciting him. She seemed to know every sensitive spot on his body, and she made them all hers with a hungry touch of possession.

"Oh, *mon chéri*, I cannot stand it any longer!" she sighed, and moved over him.

She straddled his hips. Then she guided him inside her and, pressing her inner thighs against his hips, she began to undulate, slowly at first and then faster.

Carter found her hips with his hands. His touch turned more demanding as his desire mounted, and she joined him in every movement.

She arched against him and the penetration was complete, melting, and fiery. His heated blood pulsed through his body, and a cry of pleasure burst from his lips as she matched his rhythm.

As their desire mounted, their movement increased, until finally the flames burst between them with a fierce, enthralling force.

Slowly they settled back into the soft mattress. Carter kissed her face, eyes, nose and lips, and then buried his head against her neck. For a long time they stayed that way, together, their bodies spent, pulsing, and wet. Then Carter raised up on one elbow and pushed several strands of damp hair from her face.

"You're a fascinating landlady."

She reached up and ran a finger along his jaw. "Thank you. Will you hold me all night?"

"All right," he whispered, pulling her into his arms and tugging the blankets around them.

SIX

Carter played games at the desk until he determined that Grace Wilby was still in her suite.

It was nearly noon, and the beautiful people were already gathering on the sunlit terrace to drink, see, and be seen. As an afterthought, some of them would have lunch.

Carter joined them. A hundred-franc note to an obsequious little maître d' got him a table from which he could see all: inside, the elevators, desk, and the wide stairway from the mezzanine shop; outside, the lower terrace and the pool.

He ordered a bottle of light red Figari from Corsica, and *blanquette de veau*. As he ate, he checked out his fellow diners and those on the lower terrace. None of them looked remotely like terrorists. Neither did any of the lobby loungers.

He was just finishing his salad when he spotted her at the desk handing over her key. Even with the floppy hat, the sunglasses, and the dark hair, she was easy to spot. In the light robe that barely came below her buttocks, her legs looked as if they went clear to her armpits.

Then she turned, and the effect coming head-on was even more jolting.

No, Carter thought, there were altogether too few figures that could fill out an otherwise shapeless robe like that.

Without seeming to, he followed her progress down to the pool area. She went on through the gates and down to the hotel's private beach. When she disappeared around some rocks, he shifted his attention back to the pool and the terrace. A lot of eyes followed her, but no one gave chase.

Carter finished his wine, paid, and made his way toward the beach. But instead of dropping to the sand itself, he climbed the rocks until he could see the little cove where she had spread out her towel.

She had shed the hat, the beach wrap, and her sandals. Now she stood knee-deep in the water in a three-piece bikini: two dots above, and a tiny patch of material with strings below.

She bent from the waist and splashed her body with water. When her golden-tanned flesh was glistening, she returned to the towel. With a quick flick of her fingers, she dropped the two dots from her breasts and stretched out on the towel.

Carter lit a cigarette and leaned back against a rock to watch.

The Killmaster wasn't the only one observing the sunbathing woman. A block up the beach, on the third floor of a hotel under construction, Ian Slade crouched in the cement shell with binoculars to his eyes.

Early that morning he had checked out of the Balmoral and had taken the train from Monte Carlo to Beaulieu. At the station he had checked his bags and then walked to the pink and white palace of La Réserve. After making sure that the woman was still in her suite, he had "done" the hotel.

Through observation and a rapt attention to employees'

idle chatter, Slade had found out that La Réserve was no cinch.

Day and night the security inside the hotel was tight. No one without a key could get above the mezzanine level. The service doors were electronically coded. The code had to be punched in by the employee, and each floor had its own code. If an employee's designation was the third or fourth floor, he or she could not go beyond that floor. On top of that, the whole interior of the hotel crawled with security in the halls.

There would be very little chance of getting to Constance Graves from the inside.

Ian Slade had given up on that, and shifted to the outside. It had taken the better part of the morning, but by eleven o'clock he had found the key.

That was when he had adjourned to the vacant shell of the building where he now crouched. From there he could see the windows of suite 900, and all the area behind the hotel facing the sea.

He had seen the woman have lunch on her balcony, and then watched with satisfaction as she changed into the bikini. He had followed her progress down to the beach, and now watched her nearly nude figure reclining in the sun.

It was pleasant viewing. He could see why Marcel Isban had taken her for a mistress as long as he had.

Suddenly the spectacular view was blocked by a tall, dark-haired man in a gaudy shirt. For a moment Slade thought the man would move on. But he didn't. Instead, he stretched out on the rocks, lit a cigarette, and enjoyed the view himself.

"Bastard voyeur," Slade muttered aloud.

He waited nearly an hour for the man to move. When he didn't, Slade stowed the binoculars and went back down to the street.

No matter. He would retrieve his bag and take the next train over to Nice. There he would do some shopping and find a cheap hotel.

And tonight he would return.

Carter watched her from the rocks for over an hour. When she stood and again wandered down to the water to dampen her body, he quickly undressed down to just his shirt and the swim trunks he had worn under his pants. He stuffed his clothes in the small tote bag he had purchased that morning, and moved down the rocks.

She was coming back up the sand, her heavy, bare breasts bobbing in time with her walk, when Carter hit the beach himself.

"Well, I'll be damned!" he cried, dropping his bag near her towel and jogging toward her.

"Wha . . . ?"

Two couples several paces away squinted up at them through the harsh sun. They saw nothing they hadn't seen several other times on the beach, and dropped their heads back onto their arms.

"Damn, it is you, Grace! Fancy running into you here!"

"Look, I don't—"

Carter tugged her into his arms and smothered the rest of her words with his lips. Her body, as if a button marked "automatic pilot" had been pushed in her brain, melted against his. Her arms glided around his neck, and Carter could feel every inch of her from her pillowed breasts to her knees.

When her lips started to grind a little, he tried to break the clinch, only to find her tongue hot in his mouth.

Good God, he thought, *the woman lives up to her reputation!*

At last he got her at arm's length. He held her hands,

and as he kissed them, slid the ring on her finger.

Parnoque was right. She didn't quite have both oars in the water, but she finally got it when Carter turned her hands around and held the finger with the ring directly in front of her eyes.

"Well, by Gawd, that nasty ol' bugger didn't say it'd be somethin' like you!"

She didn't bother lowering her voice, but Carter managed to cover some of it with a loud laugh.

"It's wonderful running into you like this, Grace."

"I should say," she replied, enthusiastically pressing her breast against his arm as he walked her the rest of the way to the towel.

Carter took his own towel from the bag, spread it out, and they lay on their sides facing each other.

"Please keep your voice lower than a hundred decibels," he smiled. "My name is Nick Carter."

" 'ello, Nick Carter, " she whispered petulantly. "Shall we 'ave dinner, right here at La Réserve tonight? Their lobster is bloody marvelous!"

Carter closed his eyes for a moment to concentrate. This one was not going to be any joyride.

"Miss Graves . . ."

"Connie."

"Connie . . ."

"You kiss divinely, luv."

"Thank you. Now, Connie, you told certain details to Oliver Parnoque about Marcel Isban's business dealings, right?"

"Righto, them's what I want money for. I know there're lots of folks who'd like to stick it to that bloke!"

"Well, you're right, and I'm one of them. I assume you've got what wasn't said to Parnoque?"

"That I do, luv. I got conversations in me head that I

remember, and I got pictures of papers.''

"Then all we have to do is get you talking into a tape recorder, and I'll get the film developed.''

"Wait just a minute now, luv,'' she said, arching one perfect eyebrow sharply. "What's in it for me?''

"You'll be paid what the information is worth, I assure you.''

" 'ow can I know that for sure?''

"Because you don't have anyone else who wants to buy.''

It took several seconds for that to sink in, and then she smiled broadly. "You're a sly one, ain't ya? But, luv, I gotta get fifty thousand, plus ten for Parnoque.''

"Sixty thousand dollars is a lot of money, Connie.''

"Not dollars, luv. Pounds.''

"But you paid Parnoque in dollars.''

"But *I* want to be paid in pounds.'' She ran her long fingers through the hair on his chest. "Maybe I ain't as dumb as everyone wants me to be, huh?''

Carter had to smile. Aside from everything else, there was something ingenuous about her.

"No, Connie, maybe you're not. Shall we go up to your suite and get started?''

"I think that's a right proper idea!''

She threw the robe around her without putting on her bikini top, and they started for the lobby.

"Have you noticed anyone paying special attention to you since your arrival?''

She looked at him as though *he* didn't have both oars in the water. "Look around, Nicky,'' she said with a smile.

Carter did. They were moving across the lower terrace, and every male head was following every move and jiggle she made. The fact that the thin robe kept falling open didn't help.

"I see what you mean," he groaned.

At the elevator, they were stopped by a security guard. "I'm sorry, but all guests must sign and show some identification, sir."

Carter used his own. Any doubts were wiped away by the U.S. State Department seal on his identity card.

She was all over him in the elevator, wiping out any belief of normalcy.

"Work, Connie, we've lots of *work* to do."

"So? Lordy, we got three whole days!"

"Let me ask you a question. Does Marcel Isban know how much of his business details you've got?"

"No."

"Connie, are you sure?"

That made her blink. Her little mind went to work as her teeth worried her lower lip. "I'm pretty sure."

"We'll work, Connie, as fast as possible."

Inside the suite Carter made two telephone calls, one to order up a big pot of coffee, the other to Paris AXE to have a messenger on standby in Nice.

She still hadn't moved by the time he finished. "Aren't you going to dress?"

"What for?" She gave him a demure, sidelong glance and waited for an answer.

He didn't provide one, but started to lay out the tape recorder. By the time he was set, the coffee came. As soon as the waiter was gone, he began firing questions.

She hadn't been lying. Her memory for detail—right down to verbatim, whole conversations—was uncanny. He managed to keep her talking for an hour before she started floating.

It began with pacing that ended up in front of a mirror.

"Oh, my Gawd," she moaned, throwing both palms up

to the sides of her disheveled hair dramatically, and leaning
forward to peer at her reflection in disbelief. ''Why didn't
ya tell me I looked like bloody hell? No wonder ya don't
think I've got any sex appeal.''

''Connie, I think you've got a lot of sex appeal, but—''

''Ya do? Honest?''

Carter sighed. ''What was the approximate date last year
that Isban started receiving these late-night calls every night
from Cairo?''

Slowly he got her back on the track. This time he got a
full two hours out of her before she started to fade. It was
getting dark outside.

''Gawd, my head hurts . . .''

''Just a little more, Connie.''

''And I'm hungry. Let's go down to the dining room and
'ave some dinner, eh?''

Carter sighed and punched out his cigarette. ''How much
more is there?''

''Not much, maybe a half hour at the rate we're goin'.
Can't we finish later? Me head really does hurt.''

''Okay, get the film.''

Carter reached for the phone and dialed the Nice number
that AXE Paris had given him. When the voice answered,
Carter identified himself.

''I'll meet you in the lobby of the La Réserve in fifteen
minutes,'' he said, and hung up.

Connie was back with her palms held upward. In them,
Carter counted five roles of film. ''You were a busy little
girl, weren't you?''

She grinned. ''A girl's gotta look out for herself in this
world.''

She set the film down on the coffee table and turned her
back to Carter. ''Give the shoulders a rub, will ya, luv?''
she purred, shrugging the beach jacket to the floor.

Carter used his thumbs and the tips of his fingers on her shoulders.

"Owww, feels good."

"I'll take the goods down to the messenger. Meantime, you take a shower and then I'll take you to dinner."

Abruptly she turned to face him. "You won't be long, will ya, Nicky?"

She moved his arms around her slim waist, and Carter felt the soft flesh beneath his palms quiver as her lush breasts pushed against him.

"Not long."

"Good."

Then her hands were behind his neck, tugging his face down as her mouth strained up to him. During the kiss, he thought of the previous night and the little moonlighting nurse.

There was no comparison. Constance Graves might be unbelievably beautiful, but there was no substance beneath the shell.

He patted her shoulders and turned her around. Gently he pushed her through the bathroom door. "Bathe, shower, whatever you do. I'll be back shortly."

She turned her head to look at him over a bare shoulder. "How shortly?"

"A half hour, tops."

The smile was pure Circe as the door closed behind her.

Quickly, Carter dressed. There were six tapes from the recorder. He pocketed those, along with the five rolls of film, and headed for the lobby.

Ian Slade, perched at the very top of the shell of the new hotel, breathed a sigh of relief when he saw the man leave. He was sure, for a while there, that the dark-haired man was going to bed her down and stay the night.

Slade took the steps four at a time going down, and covered the ground to the wall around the hotel in less than five minutes.

A grappling hook took him to the top of the wall. From there it was a short leap to a tall skinny fan palm. Like a monkey, with his knees pointed outward and the bottom of his sneakers gripping the palm's skin, he climbed upward.

Once he got to the very top, he started the palm swaying. Back and forth he went, until the palm was practically hitting the next one in the row. When it did, Slade curled his right arm around the second tree. Then he released and let the first tree swing back upright and stay that way.

He did this six more times, swinging like a monkey from tree to tree over the still, darkened gardens. From the last tree he swung onto the top of the huge marquee.

For a full minute he lay flat on the top of the marquee, getting his breath. Then he inched along until he reached the chain that led to the building and supported the huge sign.

He looked up when he reached it. The top of the marquee was level with the fifth floor. The chain ran up to just under the balcony of an eighth-floor suite. The wide glass doors beyond the suite were dark.

Slowly he began to climb, then faster when he was sure of his balance. Just beyond the balcony, he stood straight up. He had only to balance himself a few seconds, then fall forward.

His fingers curled around the grillwork of the balcony, and he swung himself up and over the railing. Soundlessly, he dropped into a crouch on the soft mat of outdoor carpeting.

Again he paused.

Below him, traffic crawled along the promenade. Laughing, chattering people appeared and disappeared beneath the canopy leading from the front entrance to the drive.

On the other side, a few stragglers remained in the pool

and the outside bar, and the lower terrace was starting to fill with early-evening diners.

Nowhere did he see anyone pointing up and gawking.

So far, dead solid perfect.

He swung the hard rubber grappling hook in a short arc and tossed it up and over the balcony above. When it caught on the upper railing and the line was taut, he waited to see if anyone had seen it and rushed out.

Nothing.

With another quick look below, Slade started to climb. Ten strong overhands and he was crouched outside the doors of suite 900.

Lights blazed in both the bedroom and the sitting room, but there was no sign of movement.

Slade tried the sliding door, and cursed when he found it locked. He cursed again when he saw the jamb-bar in place.

But he had come prepared.

He fashioned a crescent on the glass with masking tape, and then, from a bag at his belt, he took a battery-powered glass cutter.

Before he applied the blade, Slade put his ear flat to the glass and listened.

And then he smiled.

There was no mistaking the sound of a running shower.

SEVEN

The main lounge of La Réserve, with its oyster-white sofas, patterned floors, and Pompeian ceiling, was like the drawing room of a lavish country estate.

Carter sat in a less crowded area, partially shielded from the rest of the room by strategically placed potted palms. His eyes were alert as he studied the room and each man that entered the high, arched entrance.

It had been twenty-five minutes since the phone call. The AXE courier, Basil Johns, was late.

Carter took another sip of his beer. It was going flat and left a bad taste in his mouth. His fingertips drummed nervously on the table and he squirmed impatiently in his chair.

Then he saw Johns swing through the door, carrying a briefcase. The man paused, surveying the room. Carter stood. Johns saw him and headed over.

He was about six feet, broad-shouldered, with a lean, hard body encased in a well-cut suit. His hair, black peppered with gray, framed a darkly tanned, chiseled face. Johns was an experienced field agent. Three years before, his belly caught a round of 9mm shells in Morocco. His nerve had left him, and now he made deliveries.

He slipped into a chair opposite Carter with a tight-lipped smile. "Sorry I'm late, Nick. Traffic out of Nice on the Anglais was a bitch."

"No matter," Carter said, holding up his bottle and two fingers.

"I hate beer."

"Don't drink it," Carter replied with a chuckle. "We've got to have some reason for sitting here."

When the waiter was gone, Johns leaned forward conspiratorially. "How did you do?"

"A bonanza, I think. We won't know until the boys in Evaluation have a look."

Johns nodded. "I've a plane ready in Nice and they have a team waiting in Paris. What's it on?"

"Five rolls of undeveloped film, and six mini-cassettes. She talked her head off."

Without being asked, Johns moved his chair forward until the two men's knees touched. There were two clicks, and Carter emptied his pockets into the briefcase.

"Give me an evaluation as soon as you can."

"We'll try," Johns said, snapping the locks closed again. "What's her asking price?"

"Sixty thou . . . in British pounds."

Johns emitted a low whistle. "The lady has expensive taste."

"The lady has heavy tastes," Carter said. "Ever felt like you were about to get raped?"

The other man sighed. "Sadly, I haven't. I'll try to get back to you in four or five hours. What's your next move if it's a buy?"

"Get her out of here and out of the country. She doesn't think Isban has anyone coming after her, but I don't want to take the chance."

"Any trouble so far?"

"No," Carter replied, "but with this woman I have a hunch that trouble in always just around the corner."

"I'll be shoving off. Good luck."

They didn't shake hands. Carter waited until he was fairly sure Johns had cleared the hotel, and then headed for the elevators and the security check.

Constance Graves rose from the bubbles in the large, sunken tub. She flipped open the tub's stopper, stepped into the nearby shower stall, and revolved the spigots. The nozzle above her head gushed as the swishing sound of the water from the tub gurgled through the escape trap.

She shampooed her hair thoroughly and then rinsed it. At the same time, she thought of Nick Carter. The image of his tall, muscular body floated before her eyes as the warm water cascaded over her bare breasts. The image made her smile.

She decided she wouldn't dress for dinner right away. When he returned she would be waiting for him, still nude . . . on the bed.

Her hands were just reaching for the shower knobs when the glass door of the shower opened with a crash.

She saw two things at once: a black image, and a knife coming at her. She threw herself to the side and the blade bit into her shoulder.

The slash brought a scream of pain to her lips. More from irrational fear than calculated intent, she lunged forward. Constance Graves was a big woman, inches taller than her attacker.

Her surprise move caught Ian Slade unawares. Her shoulder slammed him full in the face, sending him sprawling through the bathroom door to the floor of the hall.

As she jumped over him, Slade slashed again, the blade leaving a gushing red line on her left buttock.

This brought another howl from the woman as she leaped over the bed toward the phone.

Slade went after her. The hand holding the phone was just coming up when Slade chopped her wrist. There was a crack as the bone broke, and then he was wrestling her to her back. He mashed his left hand over her face and lifted the knife in his right.

Through his splayed fingers, Connie saw the knife descending. She tried to scream but there was no sound.

Then there was nothing but blackness.

Bloodlust surged through Slade's body. Again and again the knife descended. Finally the fact that she was dead penetrated.

Ian Slade rolled from the body, gasping for air.

The bitch had been as strong as a man.

He looked down at his black turtleneck and trousers. They were covered with blood. It would be hell if he were spotted now.

Quickly, he snapped off the light in the bedroom and moved into the sitting room.

He was just snapping off that light when he heard the key in the door.

Carter opened the door. He was half inside before his built-in warning system went off.

It was too late.

A dark figure hurtled out of the darkness against the door, cutting off all light. Carter dived for the floor just in time to avoid a killing blow. As it was, the knife bit into his thigh.

Carter hit the parquet and immediately whiplashed his body. He caught his attacker at the knees, sending him in a dive down the three steps into the sunken living room.

Instantly the Killmaster was on his feet, groping for the light switch. He hit it and saw the short, wiry man wildly reaching for the knife he had dropped.

They both saw it at once, and dived. Only the little man changed direction. He came up on his knees and grabbed a lamp from the table beside the sofa.

As Carter came down, Slade whirled, slamming the heavy base into Carter's face. A million red lights went off and he was looking up at a foot coming at him through blood.

He managed to get his hands up in time to grasp the other man's ankle. He twisted, and the momentum sent the black-clad figure crashing into the bar. Glasses and bottles scattered everywhere, and a wall mirror shattered on the floor with a crash that would wake the dead.

Carter struggled to his feet, still groggy, wiping the blood from his eyes. He could feel that his left trouser leg was soaked, also with his own blood.

The other man was on his knees now, his arms at his back. Carter took a step forward, and the hands came forward. In them was a short-barreled revolver.

Carter ducked and spun to his left, his right leg kicking.

His foot struck the gun hand as his spin caught the other man off-balance. The explosion was like a cannon going off in the room.

The slug hit the huge pane of one of the French doors leading to the terrace, and the glass exploded.

Carter threw a chop to the man's jaw, but Slade stepped back, avoiding the blow.

Then the blood cleared enough from the Killmaster's eyes so that he could make out the killer's features.

Ian Slade. Carter knew him from a hundred photographs he had seen in years past.

Just the man's identity told him that he would have to kill him quickly or be killed himself.

Carter grabbed for the gun and managed to get Slade's wrist. The killer almost wrenched himself free, but Carter wrapped his arm around Slade's so that he held the gun hand in a hammerlock.

They struggled, Carter's back against the smaller man's chest. Then Slade smashed the heel of his free hand into Carter's face, and kept smashing.

The bastard is little, Carter thought, *but he's strong and faster than hell*. Also, he had lost a lot of blood, and was still losing.

Slowly he was losing his grip on Slade's gun hand. At the same time, he realized that the little man was maneuvering him toward the French doors and the balcony.

Carter tried to exert force in the opposite direction, but his strength had ebbed until they were about equal.

Slade maneuvered him closer and closer. Suddenly Carter lunged forward, pulling Slade off-balance. He thrust the man's hand through the shattered pane and raked it from side to side over the jagged glass.

Slade, startled, bellowed in pain. As he tried to yank his arm free, Carter put all his weight on it, slashing the arm from elbow to wrist.

Again Slade screamed, this time as much from the fountain of his own blood spewing as from the pain. His fingers opened and the gun fell to the deck of the balcony.

"Now, you little son of a bitch," Carter growled.

He grabbed Slade by the hair and threw him across the room. He went sprawling over the couch, knocked over a chair and table, and somehow ended up on his feet against the far wall.

In amazement, he held up his mutilated arm and gazed at the ripped flesh that hung in blood-dripping tatters.

He looked at Carter, then at the arm, and then back to Carter.

Like a cornered cat, his eyes blazed at the source of his pain. With a squealing scream, he charged his enemy. Again

Carter tried to evade, but the man was too fast.

He hit the Killmaster in the chest, and both of them tumbled onto the balcony. The smaller man sat on Carter's chest, his knees pinning the AXE man's arms and hands like the bite of a ferret around the throat.

Carter tried to buck him off, but he couldn't as he felt the thumb-pressure on his windpipe increase. He gasped for air and none would come. Drums started pounding in his ears as he rolled his head from side to side.

Then he spotted the revolver. He managed to get one arm free, and crawled his fingers across the thin, slick carpeting.

"Bastard, fucking bastard!" Slade was growling, the blood pumping in gushes from his shattered arm.

Then Carter's fingers found the cold steel. He stuck the barrel as far as he could into Slade's gut and pulled the trigger twice.

The sound was muffled, but the vibration from the blast slithered through the man's arms down to Carter's throat.

Then the hands were gone.

Carter flung the body away and crawled to his feet, choking for air. He was weak from loss of blood and the pounding he had taken, but he forced strength back into his body and thought back into his brain.

He staggered into the sitting room.

It was carnage. Chairs and tables overturned, lamps crushed, the bar in pieces, and blood everywhere.

And then he remembered: *Constance Graves*.

He staggered against the door. Finally it opened and he flipped the light switch.

"No!" he cried. "Goddamnit, no!"

Constance Graves was no longer beautiful. She was slumped against the headboard, in coverlets drenched with blood.

Carter moved to the bed, his own pain now forgotten.

His intent was to check her pulse.

There was no need.

Then he heard them, shouts and footsteps on the stairs. He limped back into the sitting room and put his ear to the door. Down the hall he could hear them, probably security, pounding on doors.

It would be only a matter of time before they located the suite from where all the noise had erupted.

Quickly, Carter checked the damage to his own body. It wasn't good, but it could have been worse. Most of the blood drenching his clothes was Slade's.

Then he spotted the masking tape on the partially opened portion of the balcony's door. He moved out to the balcony. Stepping over the killer's body, he found the hard rubber grappling hook still hanging from the railing.

His eyes moved. It didn't take a genius to figure out how the little killer had gotten up nine floors and inside.

"And," Carter muttered aloud, looking down at the body basking in its own blood, "if you got up here, you little bastard, I can get down."

He returned to the sitting room and got his bag. Back on the balcony, he threaded his belt through the handles and secured it to his waist.

Then he swung over the side and dropped to the eighth-floor balcony. Then he performed the same feat to get to the chain.

It was easier going down than coming up. In seconds he was on top of the marquee sign and crawling toward the end.

The hard part was throwing the pronged grappling hook and catching the skinny top of the nearest fan palm.

It took three tries before it caught and he laboriously pulled the tree toward him.

In the distance he heard the loud drone of police claxons. They spurred him to move faster. A hard-and-fast rule in the agency was to stay away from the local police . . . at any cost.

At last he was able to draw the palm close enough to climb aboard. When he let go of the marquee, the tree swung back with tremendous force, so much so that he almost reached the next tree at once. One more good sway and he made it.

By the time he reached the sixth and final tree, his wounds were bleeding again, the pressure of his exertions forcing the clots free.

He swayed the last tree over the wall, and dropped.

"Ohhh, shit," he moaned as he hit and rolled.

More blood poured from his lower lip as he bit through it from the pain.

All hell was breaking loose in the hotel now, and blue lights seemed to be flashing everywhere. But most of it was behind him. It was dark where he was in the vacant area between the hotel and a building in the distance under construction.

He managed to get to his feet and head in that direction. Twice he had to pause in the shadows of trees when he almost ran into people cutting through from the promenade to the beach for a late-night swim.

At last he reached the shell of a building, and skirted it on the ocean side. The beach was deserted and, for the most part, dark. Blindly he staggered along, his only thought for the moment putting distance between himself and the hotel.

About two hundred yards farther on, he hit another vacant lot heavy with trees and underbrush. He cut back toward the promenade and fell into a thatch of bushes six feet from the sidewalk.

What next?

If he could get to a telephone, he could call Paris. But what good would that do? Basil Johns was on a plane to

Paris. It would be hours before he could get help from that end.

And, the way he looked, there was no way he could walk the streets. He would be picked up in minutes.

Suddenly from his right there was a roar of motorcycles. There were six of them, young men with laughing girls on the back. They veered off the promenade directly across from Carter, and charged their machines up a narrow street.

Less than fifty yards up the street, they all angled into the curb and parked.

Now Carter saw them. There must have been fifty, maybe sixty motorcycles parked along the curb in front of a disco. The group that had just arrived climbed off their bikes, slid the straps of their helmets over the handlebars, and walked hand in hand into the disco.

Suddenly Carter knew where he was going and how he was getting there.

He waited until there was virtually no traffic from either direction along the promenade, and moved as fast as he could across it. Staying in the shadows, he walked from doorway to doorway up the opposite side from the disco.

The steady, pounding beat of the music seemed to shake the building's walls, and did the same for his head. He knew he only had so long now. A light film had formed over his eyes and his left leg was numb.

The bikes were parked in a haphazard row nearly the length of the block. He passed the disco and kept going. Near the end of the block a van was parked between the mass of machines and three others.

Carter crossed the street and ducked behind the van. Two of the bikes were big BMWs with front-wheel locks. The third was a small Honda with no lock and an open ignition system.

He kicked up the Honda's stand and pushed it on down

the block. Behind him he heard a burst of laughter as a group emerged from the disco.

He held his breath until he was around the corner, and then felt a surge of elation. It was downhill for a good two blocks. He swung into the saddle and coasted as far as the downhill momentum would take him. When he spotted a narrow alley, he veered into it.

Like his leg, his fingers were getting numb. It seemed to take forever with Hugo to strip the wires and reconnect them. At last he had it and kicked the machine to life. He pulled on the helmet and dropped the darkened visor. This would hide his beaten, bloody face from passing motorists. He could only hope one of them wouldn't look too closely at his clothes.

Roaring out of the alley, he cut immediately back to the promenade and turned in the direction of Nice. It would have been wiser to take the upper, less traveled road through the hills, but his vision was really foggy now, and in the extra half hour that route would take he might very well pass out.

He kept the throttle wound tight but still seemed to be crawling. He was therefore surprised when he saw the sign for Nice flash by, and then he was on the corniche leading to the port.

It took three wrong turns and ten minutes of befuddlement, but at last he found the hospital. He discarded the bike in the parking lot and lunged to the building. Thankfully, the building was empty.

He half walked, half crawled up the stairs and bounced from wall to wall down the hall to her door, where he had only the strength left to scratch instead of knock.

The door opened a crack. She saw him and it was flung wide.

"Nick . . . *mon Dieu* . . ."

"Sorry about this, Nanette, but would you mind . . ."

That's all he got out before he pitched forward into her arms and blackness.

Carter opened first one eye and then managed the other. Light streamed through the window, illuminating the walls, the ceiling. And then it came to him where he was.

He shook his head to clear the cobwebs and it nearly fell off. Instantly he closed his eyes again, and gave himself a ten count to stop everything from spinning. When it did, he opened them and looked down.

Slowly he lifted the sheet that covered him. There was a thick bandage on his left leg. His ribs were taped, and there was some kind of evil-smelling ointment on his arms and shoulders.

Then he saw the I.V. with a tube leading down to his left arm.

I'll be damned, he thought, and rolled his eyes to the other side of the bed.

She lay curled beside him on the bed, sound asleep. Gently, he removed the I.V. needle from his arm and lifted himself to a sitting position. All the aches, pains, and bruises hit at once, and he couldn't stifle a groan.

Nanette awakened instantly and sat up. "Hey, what are you doing?"

"Sitting up."

"I can see that," she replied, taking his shoulders and easing him back to the pillow, "and you're in no shape to do that."

"Just what kind of shape am I in?"

"The cut was very deep on your leg. I think you have a rib or two broken—I couldn't tell for sure. And your nose . . ."

"What about it?"

"Broken. I tried to set it." She shrugged. "I don't know how good a job I did."

"Don't worry about it. It's used to being broken. Where did you get that?" He tilted his head toward the I.V.

"From the hospital. I stole it. I also stole two pints of blood. You had lost a lot of blood. I didn't know what else to do."

"You did good," Carter groaned.

"I got your blood type from your wallet . . ."

It was there in her face—a strain—and suddenly her eyes wouldn't meet his.

"There's something else . . . what is it?" he said.

She rolled to the side of the bed and came up with a newspaper. It was all there . . . dateline Beaulieu, man and woman brutally murdered, names being withheld pending notification of next of kin . . . an American, believed to be connected to the U.S. Department of State being sought in connection . . .

"Nick . . . did you kill those people?"

Carter looked up from the paper. Her eyes were sad and her lower lip had disappeared between her teeth. She hugged herself with both arms beneath her breasts, as if she were freezing.

He made an instantaneous decision. It would be useless to lie to her now after what she had done for him.

"One of them, the man. He killed the woman, and tried to kill me. I had to kill him, Nanette."

Her shoulders lifted once and fell. "I believe you." She moved from the bed. "I will fix you some breakfast. You need solid food."

The word "breakfast" hit him. "Nanette, how long have I been out?"

"This is the morning of the second day."

"Damn. Quick, I need your phone!"

She didn't argue. She set the phone on the bed and discreetly left the room.

The moment he identified himself to the Paris office, there was a flurry of activity and David Hawk, the head of AXE, came on the line.

"Well, N3, you're in up to your ass on this one."

"I've seen the papers. They don't name me by name."

"No matter," Hawk growled. "They've got your name. We've been able to suppress it until they get your side of the story."

"I don't think you'll want me to give them my side of the story."

"Probably not," Hawk said. "I've seen pictures of the other guy. What kind of shape are you in?"

"Rough, but mobile. I've been well doctored by a nurse. What did Evaluation come up with on the goods?"

"More than we ever hoped for. The thrust has to be completely switched around now. We may have dynamite on our hands. Where are you?"

"Nice . . . just a minute . . ." He reached for and grasped Nanette's purse on the bedside stand. Rumaging, he found her wallet and opened it. "Number Four, Rue Pelère. It's just off Rue Lascaris, near a hospital. It's the third-floor apartment."

"Three hours, maybe less," Hawk said.

"It might be a good idea to use an ambulance if there's one in the motor pool."

"That can be arranged. We can take you right across the frontier in it."

"What frontier?" Carter asked.

"Switzerland. We're about to have a summit."

"Understand. One other thing . . ."

"Yes?"

"There's a woman, Nanette"—he rechecked the wallet—"Nanette Sainte. It's her flat. For security, I think she should be out of Nice for a while. Can we safe house her somewhere for a few weeks?"

"She knows?"

"Enough," Carter replied. "I think I made it here without a spotter, but it's better to be safe."

"Right. She can leave with you in the ambulance. We'll handle the rest from here. Three hours."

"We'll be ready."

Carter hung up as Nanette came back into the room with a tray. "Your people will come for you?"

"Yes. And you."

"Me?"

"It's for your own safety, Nanette. You'll be well taken care of, and compensated, I promise."

She set the tray across his lap and moved across the room to a closet. "I'll pack."

Just like that, he thought, no questions asked. *Sometimes, Carter, you just get damned lucky.*

EIGHT

The chalet was located in a remote area far from any main roads and ski trails. It was large, three stories, and sprawling. At any one time over several years it was rumored to belong to a reclusive British film star, a Persian Gulf sheik, or a South American tin mogul.

Actually, it was owned by a small American holding company in Zürich, and the company was controlled by the U.S. government. It was now—and had been for several years—an AXE-CIA safe house.

Within an hour after their arrival, Nanette Sainte had been comfortably installed in one of the third-floor bedrooms. Carter had been examined by a physician, pronounced as fit as could be expected under the circumstances, and summoned to a meeting in the billiard room, first floor.

Carter got to the library under his own power. It was a large room stuffed with ponderous books. He knew that, behind the bookcases, long-distance communications equipment and computers hummed twenty-four hours a day.

Through the library it was a right turn into the billiard room. It formed a little wing that projected out at right angles from the main body of the chalet.

Though care had been taken to make the woodwork appear old, the billiard room was obviously a modern addition. Its windows faced west. By standing at the windows, a person could look straight along the whole front façade of the chalet and observe the only road leading up the mountain.

The room was soundproof and bug resistant. The windows were bulletproof, and in cabinets behind the woodwork was an arsenal that could hold off an army. In an emergency, steel doors would seal the room off from the rest of the chalet, and it could be defended like a small fortress.

Carter limped into the room and paused. There were three men sitting around a large oval table. As one, their heads turned.

David Hawk, the grand master of AXE himelf, was the first to speak. "You look like hell."

Carter knew he did. Both eyes were charcoal-colored, and he still sported heavy bandages on his nose and forehead. His chest still bulged with bandages under the fitted shirt he wore.

"I'll live," the Killmaster replied.

"Good. Sit down before you fall down."

Carter took the one empty chair, and Hawk introduced the other two men. Carter had not personally met either of them before, but he knew both of their reputations through department files, probably just as they knew his through files in their respective agencies.

Yossele Tal was chief of Mossad's foreign operations division. He was a medium-sized man of about fifty, with a bald spot on the top of his head that he didn't try to cover up with the rest of his hair. He was nattily dressed in a dark suit, black, highly polished shoes, and a white shirt, but no tie.

Tal had eyes that bored into things, and there was an extraordinary firmness to his jaw. His voice, greeting Carter, had the timbre of power. He was one of the few men in Israeli intelligence who could make a decision without getting a go-ahead from anyone else.

Mahmoud Bey was Tal's counterpart in Cairo, with the same degree of clout. He had black eyes, a thin face, and a finely sculpted mouth across the top of which ran the narrow line of a beautifully trimmed and exceedingly black mustache. Other than lifting a cigarette to his lips with well-manicured fingers, nothing moved when he addressed Carter . . . not even his eyes.

"All right," Hawk said, "let's get to it. All three of our intelligence agencies have been sniffing out this Sons of Islam outfit for the past year. Until now we have all been working separately. As of today, that ends."

"I assume," Carter said, "that's because of Constance Graves's information?"

"You assume correctly. From the tapes and the photos, we now have enough to put a lot of pressure on the group, and on Marcel Isban. Needless to say, that will eventually be done. But we have a priority. Mahmoud?"

The Egyptian moved at last, leaning forward and resting his elbows on the table. "Through some of the documents the woman photographed, we have been able to track down the group's sudden source of funds. We had to go through a maze of companies designed to shield the source, but at last we learned a name."

While Bey talked, Hawk had been pushing buttons on a console by the table. Part of the wall slid away, and a slide projector moved up from the table's center. The lights dimmed and the projector came to life.

A broad-shouldered, handsome man with iron-gray hair and ice-blue eyes was emerging from the hatch of a small executive jet.

There was a click, and a second slide, a closeup of the previous one, appeared.

"Otto Bachman," Bey intoned. "Born in Germany, 1930, to Heinrich and Ilse von Bachman. Von Bachman senior was a rabid anti-Semite his entire life. He was one of the first members of Hitler's National Socialist Party, and stayed faithful even after the war, when he fled to Argentina."

"A war criminal?" Carter asked.

"Oddly, no. His basic job with the Reich was economics. He was a genius at funding the German war machine. Even though he was as—or more—anti-Semitic than the rest of Hitler's clan, nothing was ever proved that could connect him with the solution to Hitler's 'Jewish problem.' He was able to get to Argentina with a great deal of Nazi loot."

"And prospered under Perón," Yossele Tal added sardonically.

"That's right. He made a fortune in oil and chemicals. And along the way—until his death in 1965—he passed to his son Otto his expertise in business, as well as his hatred of Jews."

Bey paused here to open a manila folder. He selected two typewritten sheets and passed them to Carter before continuing.

"The son dropped the Von, and began to expand the family's holdings worldwide. He proved to be an even more astute business genius than his father. That list you are looking at is only a partial one. He probably openly owns or secretly controls twice that many companies."

Carter scanned the list and let a low whistle slip through his lips. "This would make him one of the richest men in the world."

"Probably. It can't be confirmed. He keeps a low profile, and since moving his base of operations to Cairo in 1980, he's more of a sportsman than mogul. His racing stable and breeding corrals produce some of the most famous horses in the world. He has brilliant managers running his international interests. Until now, we had no idea that one of his 'hobbies' was anti-Israel terrorism, but it fits.''

"And now that you know," Carter said, "isn't there any way your government can climb on his back?''

Bey lit a fresh cigarette and scowled. "No, for several reasons." He said it through tightly clenched teeth, leaving no doubt about his attitude toward his country's acceptance of Herr Otto Bachman.

David Hawk spoke up. "What you got from the Graves woman was enough to put us on the track, but not conclusive proof linking Bachman to terrorism or to the Sons of Islam.''

"Also," Bey sighed, "Otto Bachman is one of the biggest philanthropists in my country. There isn't a charity or social organization to which he doesn't contribute heavily. Couple that with the tremendous amount of wealth he generates in the country, plus the high-ranking friends he has cultivated . . .'' He paused and sighed with his hands in the air.

"I take it," Carter said, "that you want me to get this proof?''

"Something like that," Hawk said, nodding. "Without Bachman's funding, Marcel Isban and the Sons of Islam will fall back into their former dormant state. But even that isn't the big picture or the big problem now.''

"What is?" Carter asked.

Hawk nodded at Yossele Tal, and the Israeli opened the folder in front of him.

"Two weeks ago, one of our fighter-bombers was lost at sea south of Cyprus. Most of the wreckage went down. The spare fuel tanks and bits and pieces were found. Two days after the crash, the pilot—Major Isser Zail—washed ashore near Port Said. He had drowned. His only relative was a sister. She was attending school in Granada, Spain. For two days we couldn't find her. According to her roommate, she had gone off somewhere to party with a friend. Then we got a police report from the Guardia Civil. Rachel Zail had died in an auto crash near Cartagena, Spain.''

Ripples ran up the back of Carter's neck. ''Coincidence?''

''At first we accepted it as that,'' Tal replied. ''But a few days ago we received a report from one of our informants in Libya. He works the nomads in the desert south of Tobruk.''

''And . . . ?'' Carter said.

''One of his informers, the dragoman of a caravan, swears that he saw an Israeli war plane go right over his head at about two hundred feet. It just so happens that the night he claims he saw the plane was the same night Major Zail crashed in the Mediterranean Sea.''

Now the hackles really came up on Carter's neck. ''An Israeli major delivered a plane to Libya?''

Yossele Tal didn't reply directly. ''We started doing a lot of backtracking on the major and his sister. We uncovered a few things, but nothing concrete. That is, until your information tied Otto Bachman into the Sons of Islam.''

Hawk hit the change button, and a third slide came up on the screen. This one showed Bachman walking toward a stretch limousine. Directly behind him was a tall, swarthy man with curly dark hair. The second man was dressed in a well-cut summer suit, and carried two briefcases.

Another click to a closeup. The darker man had Hollywood-type good looks, and stone-cold eyes.

''Nollo Luciani,'' Mahmoud Bey declared. ''When he's not off running errands all over the world for Otto Bachman, he acts as the German's bodyguard. He's as evil as they come, from inside out. On the surface, he's beautiful.

Women follow him around with their tongues hanging out. He's from Palermo, but thanks to Bachman's connections, he now travels under an Egyptian passport. Yossele?''

The Israeli took up the story. ''As I said, we backtracked. But then, after we made the connection from your intelligence, we backtracked again. And, as you Americans say, we hit pay dirt. Four people identified Nollo Luciani as the man who accompanied Rachel Zail from a party in Granada the night she disappeared.''

Carter exhaled a cloud of smoke and leaned back in his chair with a sigh. ''Luciani kidnapped the sister, and they put the squeeze on the brother.''

''That's the only plausible explanation,'' agreed Tal. ''Isser Zail was probably wild with fright and grief. So he decided to go along with them instead of coming to us.''

''Jesus,'' Carter growled, ''and then they killed both of them.''

The projector disappeared into the table and the lights came up.

''We want you to get into Egypt, to Cairo, on a blind, and try to get close to Bachman,'' Hawk said.

''Easier said than done,'' Carter replied dryly.

''We've got a way,'' said Yossele Tal. ''For years, we've run a legit publishing company in Berlin. Now and then we assign writers to stories that may give us intelligence. We've assigned a writer to do an extended magazine piece on Otto Bachman. He's agreed.''

''I thought you said he kept a low profile,'' Carter said.

The Israeli smiled. ''Usually he does. In this case, he agreed because he admires the writer so much. Her name is Maruja Ortega.''

Carter only nodded. He didn't have to be told about Maruja Ortega. She was a fire-breathing, one-sided journalist from Madrid. She made no bones about being anti-Zionist and pro-Fascist. Her biggest hero was Franco, and she did at least one piece a year devoted to keeping his memory alive.

It was easy to see how Bachman would have a lot of respect for Maruja Ortega. If any journalist could get close to him, she could.

"You mean," Carter asked, "you're sending me in on her coattails?"

"In a way," Tal chuckled. "You see, we have used Ortega for many assignments. She has no inkling, of course, that her real employers are Israeli intelligence. For nearly two years now, Ortega's personal secretary has been Ruth Melzer."

"And she's yours." Carter grinned.

Tal nodded. "She's blond, blue-eyed, fair-skinned—about as Aryan as you'd want. She was born in Wiesbaden and carries a German passport. She is also a Jew, and has been a Mossad agent for twelve years."

"Where do I fit?" Carter asked.

Hawk shoved identity papers, a German passport, a driver's license—an entire life—across the table. All in the name of one Bruno Dietrich.

"Until three weeks ago, there really was a Bruno Dietrich. He was a small-time arms dealer and sold a lot of goods to a dozen or more terrorist groups, including the Sons of Islam."

"And now . . . ?"

"He was on the run," Hawk replied. "The BfV caught up with him in Mannheim. He tried to blow his way out, and bought it. German intelligence kept his death a secret in case they could use him some day. He's a gift to us."

Carter concentrated on the papers. They were already laid

out with his picture. "My German is flawless, but what about Isban and his people? They know me. They've already tried for me once in London ."

Mahmoud Bey chimed in. "There is very little chance that any of the Sons of Islam members will be around Bachman in person. It would be too risky for his image. You'll go in as a former lover of Ruth Melzer and a man on the run. I'll personally be your contact in Cairo, and your escape valve. Also, in my agency I have people who are loyal to me to a fault. We can give you backup. What do you say, Mr. Carter?"

The Killmaster shrugged. "Sounds like a piece of cake. When do I leave and how do I get there?"

Hawk produced airline tickets and a travel brochure. "Maruja Ortega is deathly afraid to fly. She and Ruth Melzer are taking the Greek Sun Line cruise aboard the *Stella Solaris* day after tomorrow from Piraeus, to Alexandria. From there, they train to Cairo."

"Where do I contact Melzer?"

"At the King's Palace in Athens. She and Ortega have adjoining suites."

"The secretary rates a suite?" Carter asked.

Hawk nodded. "Ortega travels in style, as does everyone in her party."

"It's part of her contract," Yossele Tal said dryly. "We pay for it."

Carter stood and gathered all his credentials. "I'll need a wardrobe. I'd better get hopping."

"Mr. Carter . . ." It was Tal.

"Yes?"

Tal handed Carter a slip of paper. "I know I need not stress the importance of this. If there is an Israeli fighter-bomber out there in the desert somewhere, we want it back or destroyed. Those are the activating codes for the jet's self-destruct system. We would also like to know why they grabbed it in the first place."

Carter only nodded.

What could he say?

He had already muffed one and gotten Constance Graves killed. He sure as hell didn't want to muff another one.

NINE

He was a pig, and drunk. He had two chins, fat jowls, and smelled of ouzo, both from his breath and his tie where he had spilled part of the drink.

Twice he had tried to pick her up in the bar, and twice she had politely tried to tell him to kiss off. Now he was following her to the elevator.

Ruth Melzer cursed herself for stopping in the hotel lounge for a drink instead of having one from the mini-bar in her room. But it had been a rough day. Maruja had been more than her usual bitchy self. To make matters worse, the woman had said that reservations might be needed for two friends from Paris on the ship. And now they had saddled her with an American agent who was supposed to pass for German.

God, the Americans! Why hadn't they just let her handle it?

Floppy Jowls moved close to her in the elevator, close enough to make her glasses foggy.

"Ah, pretty blond lady, I tell you I know a restaurant that is only fit for the gods . . ."

"I'm afraid I'm very mortal."

"You must eat, I must eat. Why not eat together?"

"Your leg is against my leg."

"I know. In this restaurant you will taste the best of Greece . . . *moussaka*, *dolmathes*, and *tiropita* that will make you cry! You like the fruits of the sea?"

"Your hand is on my ass."

"You will taste the wonders of *ktenia* and *achivades pilafi*—that's scallops and clams over rice—and a *baklava* so light it is fit for the gods of Olympus . . ."

"For the last time, buster, get your hand off my ass."

"Then it is back to my villa for strong, sweet coffee . . . the only good thing to come from the Turks. *Ahhhh!*"

She was using both hands between his legs on his testicles. First she ground them together, bringing the scream. Then she yanked them hard, then hard again, bringing tears to his eyes. When the elevator stopped on her floor, she made a fist of one hand and tried jamming them all the way back up into his belly.

He passed out and slid to the floor.

"Good night," she said and smiled sweetly, then she punched the button for the top floor as she stepped from the elevator.

Damned stupid thing to do, Ruth thought as she let herself into her suite, *but the bastard deserved it*.

She dropped her purse on a chair and walked into the bedroom. In the bath, she turned on the water in the tub and, back in the bedroom, kicked off her shoes. She fumbled at the side zipper of her skirt. When it parted, she released it to let it slide over her hips to the floor.

She stepped from it and, tossing her heavy blond hair, lit a cigarette from a pack on the dresser.

Then, clad only in bra and black bikini panties, she moved

into the sitting room to the mini-bar. She fixed a drink, neat, swallowed half of it, and, with a swift bending of her supple body, shed her underwear.

The bare flesh, pink and gleaming against the darker areas of tan, was beautiful. Her breasts were full, ripe, and stood out firmly. They were a delightful counterpoint to the flat plane of her stomach, the flare of her hips, and the graceful tapering of her legs.

"So sorry. Really didn't mean to drop in on you while you were . . ."

The voice was a soft baritone speaking perfect German. Ruth barely saw him—tall, wide-shouldered—before she launched herself at him.

She managed to get one hand on his throat and start the other up for a blow, when she was lifted from the floor by a fist in her stomach. She came down on the sofa in a very indelicate pose, gasping for air with the room swimming in front of her eyes.

She saw him disappear into the bedroom. He returned with her robe and draped it over her.

"Terribly sorry, but I did try to apologize in the first place."

Ruth tried to say something, but there was no air to say it with. He moved to the bar, fixed himself a drink, and returned with hers.

Bastard, she thought, *cocky bastard!*

He set her drink and cigarette in front of her, then took the opposite chair.

He never took his eyes from her, and his smile never faded. She noted now that his nose was covered with white adhesive tape, and that he had dark, purple bruises around his deep-set brown eyes.

In spite of this, he was unusually handsome, in a crude

sort of way. She cursed herself for having that thought, and found her voice.

"How did you get in here?" she demanded. "And just who the hell are you?"

The tall stranger grinned. "Over the balcony. I have the next suite. I thought it would be easier to be lovers if we were close."

Ruth had been trying to sip her drink. Now she gagged. She was pretty sure she already knew, but she asked anyway.

"Then you're . . . ?"

Carter held out his hand. "Bruno Dietrich." The smile, even with a puffy lip, still managed to be charming.

"Oh, God." She managed to get some of the drink down, not acknowledging his hand. "Weren't there easier ways?"

"Not really. I thought it best to talk to you first, before meeting Maruja Ortega."

Now Ruth Melzer studied him coolly. Other than the rugged face and the gnarled hands, he did not look like someone who could kill. But she had been told that he was their best, a seasoned veteran who had come through so many wars that he had been dubbed the Killmaster.

Then she realized that the robe he had thrown over her didn't cover all of her. Hastily she turned away, got into the robe, and belted it. As she did, she watched him over her shoulder.

That was when she caught cold steel in his eyes and knew that he hadn't even noticed her nudity.

She shivered slightly and again took her seat.

"Cold?"

"No," she replied, taking her drink and pulling her legs up underneath her on the sofa. "Why didn't you just use the telephone?"

The broad shoulders moved in a shrug. "La Ortega might

have been with you. It could have been awkward.'' His mouth curled in something resembling a sardonic smile. ''I get the feeling you aren't happy with a coconspirator?''

''I'm not. Ortega is enough to handle without handling you, too.''

The smile faded and the face became granite. ''I assure you, Fräulein Melzer, I can handle myself. Now, let's dispense with this surreptitious cow dung. Did Maruja Ortega accept your story about me and my situation?''

''I think so, yes,'' she replied, forcing herself to stay calm, to keep her temper down. ''I told her we had been lovers—that you were running from the West German police on a charge of running guns to terrorists.''

''Did she buy it?''

''Yes. She loves being close to dangerous people. It seems to galvanize her hormones.''

''Good. Am I on the ship?''

Ruth rose, crossed the room to her purse, and returned. ''Here are your travel documents . . . the voucher for your stateroom, and your seating for dinner. I've put you with me, of course, at dinner.''

''Of course.'' The smile came back. ''And the stateroom?''

She froze. ''We are *ex*-lovers, remember? We stay that way. You are on the opposite side of the ship from Maruja and me. This is business to me, just business.''

''What did you think I was suggesting?''

She snorted. ''I know what you will eventually suggest. I've met Americans before . . . your type. It is perhaps just as well that you understand now that I have no interest in fornication, with you or any other man.''

''Fornication?'' Carter said, unable to suppress a widening of the smile.

"Fucking."

"Yes, I know. Well, I'm glad we've gotten that out of the way."

"These things are better understood immediately."

"Dear Ruth, you have no heart."

"The heart," she replied curtly, "has the sole function of distributing the blood through the body."

"Dear Ruth, you also have no sense of humor," Carter said, finishing his drink and returning the glass to the bar.

In a mirror above the mini-bar, he watched her. The smooth, modulated voice, the cool, classic beauty of her face, the lovely body, and the detached sophistication. It all boiled down to something cold, and repellent.

He spoke without turning. "For Ortega to accept me through you, you're going to have to be very sweet to me in front of her."

"I know that."

"She must think that our love affair is still very much alive."

"I know that as well," she replied, a little flame of anger flaring in her clear blue eyes.

Carter moved back across the room to stand over her. "While we're at it, let's get something else straight."

She stood, tightening the belt of the robe around her. "I'm listening."

She was standing close to him. Near enough for him to be aware of the sweet, sharp smell of her body, the wet brilliance of her eyes. She was a beautiful, desirable woman, but Carter didn't let that thought show in his eyes or on his face.

"Yossele Tal sent me in because you're not equipped to handle the end result of this situation. If that hurts your ego, that's tough. You'll do what I say, when I say it. And when the time comes for you to get out of the way, that's exactly what you'll do. Have you got that?''

A white line appeared along her jaw. "Yes, I've got that."

Carter smiled. "That's good."

Suddenly, both hands came out to capture her. He pulled her to him and kissed her brutally. When she began twisting her head from side to side, he wound the fingers of one hand in her blond hair and held her still so that she couldn't twist her face away.

His left hand tightened at her back, crushing her breasts to his chest. He felt her knees give a little, and ground his lips harder over hers.

When he was satisfied, he released her. She fell back to the sofa, gasping.

"Not bad," he growled. "But you'll have to do better when the time comes."

Without another word, he moved to the balcony and disappeared.

Of the three *Stella* ships on the Sun Line, the *Stella Solaris* was the largest and by far the most opulent. Of the five cabin decks, the Boat deck itself was top-drawer.

Carter wasn't surprised to discover that he had a private suite on the Boat deck. Maruja Ortega and Ruth Melzer had adjoining suites on the opposite side of the ship. Checking the price in the brochure brought a smile to his lips.

No wonder Yossele Tal had dryly remarked that Ortega traveled first class and the Mossad paid for it.

Embarkation began at three o'clock. Carter boarded at four. By five he had unpacked and changed into cool summer whites. He was sipping a scotch from the bottle he had requested from the steward upon boarding, when there was a light rap on his door.

It was Ruth Melzer, casually ravishing in a simple white linen dress that accented her figure but didn't advertise it.

Her blond hair was done in old-fashioned Bavarian braids, and her blue eyes had the cool outdoor look of ski runs and bottomless mountain lakes in them.

"May I come in?"

"Of course. Drink?"

"Some wine?"

"Scotch."

"No, thank you," she said, sitting on the very edge of a large couch. "You are invited to join us in the forward lounge for a drink before sailing."

"When?"

"Now . . . or in a few minutes. Before we go, I would like to brief you on a few things."

"Such as?"

"Maruja doesn't speak German. She hates it when people speak and she doesn't understand."

"You're saying, don't speak German," Carter said.

"Right. English will do."

"I'm also fluent in Spanish."

Her eyes rounded a little. "All the better," she said grudgingly. "There is one other thing that could be important. It's a personal trait of hers . . ."

"Yes?"

"She knows your background. I've told her about it, as well as the circumstances of your running. Besides being intrigued by people like you . . ."

"Dangerous people?"

"Um, yes," she said, allowing a slight smile to soften her features. "She also has a tendency . . . well, it's like a game with her, to . . ."

"Yes?" Carter said, now suppressing an outright belly laugh.

"Well, it's a game she plays. Often it's as if she competes with me . . ."

"Are you saying that she'll probably try to get me into bed?"

"Yes, dammit." She stood, a flush suffusing her cheeks.

"Well, well," Carter chuckled, "that should be jolly fun. Shall we go?"

In the passageway, he put an arm possessively around her waist. She tensed, but she didn't move away.

Carter followed her through the main lounge to the Class A tables overlooking the bow. The whole was sumptuous in autumn reds and brown velvets, highlighted with lots of leather and bronze.

It was nearly full, with well-dressed people sitting over cocktails and talking softly. Now and then a woman's clear laughter would ring out.

The table was reserved in Ortega's name. Carter ordered, and the drinks appeared within seconds.

"Know anyone?" he asked, perusing the crowd.

"Quite a few, actually," Ruth replied. "It's that time of year. This is the kind of crowd Maruja loves to travel with. There she is."

Carter swiveled in his chair. He had only heard of Maruja Ortega, never seen her, not even a picture. Now he was shocked.

She had entered the lounge and paused, looking for the table. By any standards she was a raving beauty. Carter knew her age to be close to fifty, but she looked to be in her middle thirties. She was tall and aristocratic, with dark auburn hair pulled back in a chignon from a Botticelli face dominated by enormous dark eyes.

The dress was a radiant blue, and cut low enough to leave very little of her magnificent bosom to the imagination.

She spotted Ruth and moved forward. As she traversed the room, she waved to several expensive-looking people

with the gay and professional expertise of an actress making
an entrance. Now and then she paused to proffer a verbal
greeting.

"Well, well," Carter murmured, and stood as the appa-
rition reached the table.

"Hello," came a husky voice unnervingly directed at Carter. "You are, of course, Ruth's gentleman."

"Mine, until now," Ruth said with a laugh.

A point for you, Ruthie dear, Carter thought, holding
Maruja's chair. He bowed to her hand, clicking his heels
slightly.

"Bruno Dietrich, Señorita Ortega. I cannot tell you how
much I have admired your work." He spoke in fluent
Spanish, and it obviously had the desired effect.

"You speak Spanish," she said with a smile, her eyes
sparkling with obvious approval. "How wonderful. Ruth
didn't tell me."

Carter returned the smile. "I'm sure there are many things
about me she did not tell you."

"I must admit I was reluctant to say yes when Ruth asked
me if you could accompany us to Cairo, but now I'm so
glad I did. Did you have an accident?"

Carter touched the bandages at his face. "An automobile.
Nothing serious."

"Good, I'm glad."

As she spoke, she leaned forward and squeezed Carter's
hand. It was impossible to avoid the view. The neckline of
her dress seemed perilously suspended, its contents about
to find freedom.

Carter saw a frown crease Ruth Melzer's forehead, and
upped his own charm quotient twenty-two points.

They chattered through two drinks. Maruja Ortega was
an erudite woman, but at this moment her conversation was
clipped, with a meaningless context. Carter sensed some-

thing questioning, alert, even wary in her attitude. The atmosphere of acceptance she had so quickly established at their initial meeting suddenly became a clever armor or shield, impregnable to the threat of any genuine intimacy.

His mind had begun to wander as Maruja chattered on. A comment by Ruth brought him back to the conversation.

"You are, of course, the boss, Maruja, but I think it is presumptuous of you to use your influence with Herr Bachman for a nightclub singer."

"Nonsense. My articles will make the man so famous, and Clothilde will draw so many people into his club, that he will be kissing my foot thanking me. Oh, here they come now!"

It was then that Carter spotted the two conspicuously empty chairs at the table, and followed the two women's line of sight.

The woman under discussion was approaching the table with a small, darkly handsome man.

She was a thin young woman, pale and wan, wearing a somewhat ill-fitting black dress. There were lines of strain between her eyes, and when she was introduced to Carter she avoided his gaze. She seemed uncomfortable and almost painfully ill at ease.

"And, Bruno, this is Clothilde's husband, Monsieur Zayak Boudia."

"So happy to meet you, Monsieur Dietrich."

The conversation had slipped automatically into French. Carter said about the same in response, and shook the man's hand.

While they had another drink, the *Stella Solaris* slipped from its dock and glided into the Mediterranean.

As the moon came up and the conversation continued, the young wife clutched a handkerchief in her right hand. Her fingers were wrapped tightly around it.

But, for the moment, Carter was more interested in her husband, Zavak Boudia. A little bell had gone off in Carter's head when he first saw him. He was sure that he had either met the man before or he had seen the face. Now the little bell had becoming a clanging dirge, but he still couldn't pin the man down.

The announcement came for first seating for dinner, and Maruja Ortega led the way, with the young married couple on her arms.

Carter, with Ruth's arm in his, dropped back a few paces.

"Well, congratulations," she murmured. "You seem to be a tremendous hit with Maruja."

"Oh? I wouldn't be too sure. What's with the lovebirds?"

She sighed. "Maruja dropped that bomb on me just yesterday. I almost went crazy getting them a suite."

"Who are they?"

"Clothilde is a singer in a Paris club. Maruja heard her a couple of months ago at a private cocktail party. She's enchanted with her, and thinks exposure in a major club, like the Aladdin's Lamp in Cairo, will boost her career."

"What about the husband, Zayak?"

Ruth shrugged. "Don't know. He's Lebanese, married Clothilde about a month ago. Why?"

"I'm not sure . . . yet. You say you really had to work to get them space on the ship?"

"Yes. As I said, it was short notice. Maruja gave me no inkling she was sponsoring Clothilde into Egypt until yesterday morning."

"What about their visas? Did you get those, too?"

"No," she replied. "I wasn't asked."

"Find out where and when they got them. Can you do that?"

"I suppose so. I'll have to make out the list for Egyptian customs eventually. I'll just do it tonight instead of later."

"Good. When you find out, I'll be in my suite."

Dinner was more of the same inane chatter, with Maruja Ortega leading it. The young couple said barely a word, and Ruth played yes-girl to her boss.

Carter continued to lay on the charm, and by the time the meal was over, Maruja Ortega was not only eating out of his hand, she was resting her hand on his leg.

He decided he may have taken it a little too far too fast, and excused himself over brandy.

It was nearly midnight when the knock came on the door. He was sure it was Ruth with the visa information. But when Carter opened it, he was smiling at the wrong lady.

"Buy a lady a nightcap?"

Maruja Ortega glided by him in something very gossamer and very expensive.

"Of course." He moved to the mini-bar. "Scotch?"

"That will do," she said, gliding to the sofa and oozing seductively down into its cushions. "Ruth has told me all about your exciting life. I couldn't really ask you any questions at dinner, but I'm dying to hear it from your own lips."

As Carter passed her the drink and joined her on the sofa, he tried to read beyond the blazing smile and the probing eyes.

"It's really not that exciting."

"Nonsense. She said that for years you smuggled arms to our Palestinian brothers. Tell me all about it . . . I must know!"

He talked. She asked questions, and he answered them from the nine-page dossier on Bruno Dietrich he had memorized in Switzerland.

And while he talked, he tried to cut through the myriad layers of Maruja Ortega. At the end of the hour, he was no further along that when he started.

He couldn't tell if she was trying to get him into bed, or

just talk. Neither could he ascertain if her interest was of an interview nature or an interrogation.

Finally he decided to become the aggressor. His hand found her shoulder and then moved down her back. She caught it, held it, and asked more questions.

Carter gave her more pat answers and slid closer. When the moment was right, he took her in his arms.

"Maruja, do you realize how exciting and beautiful a woman you are?"

"Thank you, but . . ."

She tried to wriggle away, but Carter held her tighter. When he kissed her, he found her hands firmly on his chest.

"Why are you afraid of me?" he murmured.

She laughed sharply. "Afraid? How absurd. On the contrary, I find you intriguing."

He was about to kiss her again, when there was a knock.

"Ah-ha," she said with a smile, and then whispered, "that will be Ruth. She told me also that you were lovers."

Skillfully she maneuvered out of his arms, glided to the door, and opened it.

"Ruth, my dear," she said, almost coyly, "I thought you would be saying good night. You're right, he is fascinating. Some time, when he is completely out of danger, I'll have to write his life story. Well, good night, you two!"

She practically tugged Ruth into the room and stepped into the passageway. Then she leaned back in and whispered loudly enough for Carter to hear, "I won't need you until noon tomorrow, darling. Have a fantastic night!"

Then the door was closed and she was gone. Ruth Melzer turned, wide-eyed, to Carter.

"What in the world was that all about?"

"I think," he replied, "that I have just been thoroughly interrogated."

One eyebrow shot up. "You're wearing lipstick."

"I know," he said, frowning at the door. "I tried to get her into bed."

"You did?"

"I did my best, and she would have none of it."

"Well," Ruth shrugged, "that's a new wrinkle. I got the information you wanted."

"Good," he said, peeling out of his shirt. "Start talking."

"The Boudias were married only recently. Not even a month ago, as I had thought, but last week. In fact, Clothilde didn't have time to get a new passport. The one she carries is still in her maiden name, Irion. She had to pencil in her married name."

"And the visas for Egypt?"

"Both issued at the Egyptian embassy in Paris two days ago. And that's what's odd."

"What?"

"I saw their receipted copy of the visa request. They had left it in the envelope with their papers."

"And?"

"The visas were requested at nine o'clock in the morning, and granted at ten."

That got Carter's attention. "That's a little fast, isn't it?"

Ruth nodded. "About eight days too fast. Egyptian bureaucracy just doesn't work that quickly."

"They must have had something—or someone—on the other end working for them."

"Isn't that a little odd, for a singer and her husband?"

"You bet your cute little bottom it is," he growled. "I'll check it when I make my report to Yossele Tal's contact at the Rhodes stop tomorrow." He dropped his pants and started to hang them up.

"What are you doing?"

"Getting ready for bed," he replied. "As you should do. It's late, and tomorrow will be very busy."

"God, you are rude *and* crude," she snapped, and started for the door.

"Where are you going?"

"Back to my stateroom."

"Are you dense?" he said sharply. "You heard La Ortega. She doesn't need you until noon. She knows we were lovers. She told you to have a fantastic night. What will she think if you trot back to your room at this hour?"

Her lip began to quiver and her body shook visibly. "You mean, I have to stay here?"

"I think it would be wise until a decent hour . . . say, dawn?"

"Damn!" she cried. Carter dropped his shorts. "What are you doing?"

"I sleep naked," he announced, grinning, and crawled into the bed.

"Well, I'm not sleeping with you!"

"Fine. I'm sure you have a strong back. Sleep on the couch. Turn out the lights, will you?"

She had been speaking English. Now she reverted to her native German. Carter smiled into the pillow. Even he couldn't swear with such glibness in that tongue.

Eventually she settled down and in anger stomped around the suite turning off the overhead lights, leaving only a night light shining through the open bathroom door.

From the closet she got a light coverlet and threw it on the couch. She kicked off her shoes and slipped out of her dress and pantyhose. She had just released her bra and was shrugging out of it, when she saw one of Carter's eyes wide open and gleaming at her in the illumination from the night light.

"Bastard." She slammed the bathroom door.

"I have seen you naked before."

"Shut up."

"Good night."

She didn't reply. He heard her settle into the couch, and settled in himself. He heard her toss, then turn, then toss some more. She groaned, cursed, and then some more tossing.

There was a curve in the couch just about where her hips would be.

He gave her a half hour.

It took twenty minutes by the illuminated dial on the bedside clock.

He heard her feet hit the floor and then pad across to the bed. He felt her weight come down, and then there was a full three minutes of frenzied activity.

Carefully, he reached out his hand. He felt, in turn, the blanket and pillows from the couch, two of the three pillows from her side of the bed, and the bottoms of both chairs.

"What in God's name are you doing?" he growled.

"Making a bundling board. Good night!"

Carter laughed himself to sleep.

TEN

The *Stella Solaris* docked at its first port of call, the Greek island of Rhodes, at ten sharp the following morning. Carter waited until there was a mass of humanity moving down toward the gangway, and inserted himself in the center of them.

He meandered aimlessly around the streets near the port for a half hour, until he was sure he had shed all his fellow passengers, and then found a cab.

"Lindos."

"Lindos? You can walk," the driver stated.

"I know," Carter replied, settling back in the rear seat, "but I'm lazy and I want to go by the inland road."

"That will cost you double."

"Besides being lazy, I am rich."

It was a pleasant drive over the island of roses, the legendary home of the sun god Apollo, and Carter let himself relax and take in the beauty.

By the Acropolis at Lindos he called a halt. "Wait for me," he instructed the driver. "I'll meet you in that little taverna there, at the corner."

"*Wait* for you?" The driver was irate. "Are you crazy?"

"Yes," Carter said, dropping an American one-hundred-dollar bill on the seat. "Wait."

"Until the gods come down from Olympus," said the driver cheerfully. "Have a nice day."

Carter headed for the older part of the little whitewashed town, and found the street—actually little more than an alley—in less than half an hour.

The building was only five stories, but since it housed men of the professions, it sported an elevator. Or rather a reasonable facsimile: three by three, with a cage and an old man with watery eyes and a cap on his head that said "Guardian" in Greek.

"I'm looking for the lawyer, Tomopoles. Has he arrived yet?"

The old man nodded sleepily, and closing the outer wire gate but leaving the inner one open, he sent the cage lurching upward.

"Anyone ever been killed in this?" Carter asked casually.

No answer.

At the fifth floor he stopped the elevator and opened the gate. Tomopoles's office door faced the elevator. There was more than natural light coming through the frosted pane of the door.

Carter opened the door into a tiny outer office. There was a secretary's desk sporting a typewriter. The machine had cobwebs running from its cover to the top of the desk.

The Killmaster knocked, heard a grunt, and, interpreting that as a signal to enter, went into the inner office.

Constantin Tomopoles was an old man with a yellow, bloated face and nearly colorless eyes. Under the eyes were unhealthy, oyster-colored pads. His hair had long ago faded from black to a yellowish white. It was plastered down and a part neatly bisected his scalp. He wore a brown suit that hadn't seen the steam of a presser since the Nazi occupation.

"What?" he asked in slurred Greek.

There was one window, behind the desk and the slouching man, that overlooked the alley, the main street, and the sea in the distance. Carter dropped his Bruno Dietrich passport on the desk and moved to the window.

It was clear. Not that he expected to see anything out of the ordinary, but Maruja Ortega's interrogation instead of seduction the previous night had set more bells off in his suspicious mind.

"You're early," came the old man's raspy voice. "Do you have a word for me?"

"Tal," Carter said, and turned from the window.

The office furniture could be inventoried in a single glance: one desk, mahogany-stained with peeling veneer; two chairs, same color and hard as rocks; one sink and mirror, both cracked; and one filing cabinet as cobwebby as the typewriter in the outer office.

"Is this the best cover they'll give you?"

Tomopoles shrugged. "Siphoning off from expenses gives me more income. I'm a poor man. I do my job."

"You probably own half of Rhodes," Carter growled, moving around the desk and taking one of the hard chairs.

"Perhaps a third," the old man said, belching and putting a mint in his mouth. "They said you were American."

"I am."

"Your Greek is good."

"Thank you. What have you got for me?"

Tomopoles leaned forward, wheezing, and Carter noticed that he had a pulpy nose crisscrossed with purple veins. "I had a transmission last night, and three more this morning. Nearly all the cells of the Sons of Islam have been pinned down, as well as their members. Of course, there has been no move against them. It is thought that any disruption now could jeopardize your mission."

"Where is the largest concentration?"

"About half and half between Europe and the Middle East. What is most important is that yesterday started a migration."

"From where to where?"

"From? . . . everywhere. To? . . . Yemen, northern Ethiopia, Port Sudan, the Gulf of Suez. Even those members in Israel are moving south to Eilat."

Carter put his fingers to his temples and closed his eyes, conjuring up a map of the Middle East. At last he spoke.

"They are converging on the Red Sea."

Tomopoles wheezed. It made so much noise that Carter expected it to be visible, like a green cloud. "It would seem so."

"But why? Why suddenly a mass of them along the Red Sea?"

The man slid another mint into his mouth and chewed it in silence for a moment. When he spoke again, there seemed to be a hint of relief in his voice.

"I'm a Greek. I know nothing of the desert or the Moslems who run wild in it."

"Of course," Carter sighed. "Anything else?"

A slip of paper came his way across the desk. "Your place of contact in Alexandria, and times. Burn that when you memorize it."

Carter glanced at the paper once, set it in an ashtray, and put his lighter to it.

"I want you to pass on a bio request, complete."

"Of course." A pudgy hand took up a pencil and poised its tip over a pad.

"A recently married couple, Clothilde and Zayak Boudia. She's French; he is originally Lebanese. They are both traveling under French passports. Her maiden name was

Irion. Also, she's some kind of a singer, works clubs in Paris.''

''Is that all?''

''Not quite.'' Carter reiterated the circumstances of their Egyptian visas. ''I'd like to know the Cairo authorization.''

''I'll pass it on immediately. Anything else?''

Carter stood. ''That's it. Tell me, Tomopoles, why do you work for the Israelis?''

This time a grin before the wheeze. ''Besides paying very well and offering the best protection, my wife was an Israeli. I met her in Haifa.''

Carter smiled. ''Give her my regards.''

The smile disappeared. ''I would if I could. She was killed in a terrorist attack on the Golan Heights while visiting her mother three years ago.''

Carter left feeling much better about Constantin Tomopoles. A man who worked such a dangerous game for money alone was dangerous.

Carter returned to the ship in time for late lunch. On the way to the dining salon he stopped by the bar. Zayak Boudia was seated alone near the entrance. When Carter headed his way, the man nodded a curt greeting and abruptly left.

Just antisocial, Carter wondered, or was there something more?

He lunched, found an *International Herald Tribune*, and went out on the Lido deck to sit by the pool. Even though a high percentage of the passengers had gone ashore to sightsee on Rhodes, there were still a lot of sun-worshiping ladies around the pool. More than one of them flashed him a smile.

Rejecting his baser instincts, Carter found a lounge and opened the paper. He was a third through the sports section when a shadow fell over the pages.

He looked up into the face of a young man in well-tailored tweeds and a fez. His eyes were bright and sharp, and he carried a clipboard thick with papers.

"Herr Bruno Dietrich?"

'Yes.''

"I am Omar Azia, of the Egyptian Tourist Authority. If it is not inconvenient, I would like to ask you a few questions."

"Of course. Sit down."

"Thank you. A matter of routine, you understand." He sat and thumbed through the papers. "You are not taking the entire *Solaris* tour?"

"No, I'm getting off in Alexandria with the Ortega party."

"Yes, I have a note of that. Your reasons for visiting Cairo?"

"Sun, fun, the Pyramids, the Sphinx."

"Your health." The irony was in the eyes and the smile.

Carter matched the smile but felt a tension sift through his body. "Perhaps."

"And you'll be staying at Shepheard's?"

"That's what I put on the card."

"A fine old hotel, full of memories and nostalgia."

"Of better times," Carter said, openly referring to colonial times when Egypt was under British rule and Shepheard's was where the colonials congregated.

The smile got downright oily. "That, of course, is a matter of opinion."

"Of course," Carter replied dryly.

"How long do you plan on visiting Cairo?"

Carter shrugged. "A few days."

The dark eyes studied him openly. "I will be blunt, Herr Dietrich."

"Please."

"Your reputation is rather spotty. In fact, Interpol has quite an extensive dossier on you."

"Is that right?"

"You know it is. We would appreciate it if, while you are in Cairo, you confine yourself to only tourism."

"I'll keep that in mind," Carter said.

The young man stood. "Thank you for your cooperation. You understand that we are not singling you out. Every visa is checked thoroughly. It is an unfortunate sign of the times. Have a nice stay in Cairo."

He moved away and Carter muttered "Bullshit" under his breath.

Someone in the Egyptian government besides Mahmoud Bey was very interested in him. He wondered if it was the same person who had rushed Clothilde and Zayak Boudia's visas through.

The *Stella Solaris* left Rhodes at five that evening. Arrival in Alexandria was scheduled for six the next evening. Carter pretty much hibernated in his cabin, but he did manage lunch the next day alone with Ruth Melzer.

"Maruja got a cable this morning from Bachman. His Rolls is picking us up in Alexandria the morning after we arrive, to take us to Cairo. She sends her regrets but there won't be room enough for five and luggage in the car."

"I see. So I still take the train to Cairo?"

"Yes. Also, she and I will be staying at Bachman's villa there."

"And the happy newlyweds?"

"Like you, they will be staying at Shepheard's. I made sure that you will be my escort at any of the functions at the villa."

"Good. I can still get close to Bachman if I play my

cards right. Communication with you might be a little tricky, but—''

''No, that shouldn't be a problem,'' she said.

''Oh?''

''Maruja has given me my nights free. She . . .'' Ruth paused, color suffusing her cheeks.

''Yes?'' Carter prompted.

''She intimated that I could spend them at Shepheard's.''

Now Carter smiled openly, remembering the morning they had awakened together. During the night, the bundling board Ruth had so carefully erected had disappeared and she had bolted awake in his arms.

''To satisfy your carnal desires,'' he chuckled.

''That's what she hinted at,'' Ruth said dryly. ''If we get separated getting off the ship, I'll see you at the hotel in Alexandria. I've made reservations for all of us at the Maamura Palace.''

''I'll look forward to it,'' Carter said, brushing the back of her hand with his lips.

Even at six in the evening, the great sprawling city of Alexandria lay under an oppressive haze of heat. Even the water sluicing around the hull of the great liner as it docked at the pier seemed to hiss with steam instead of froth.

Carter managed to avoid the Ortega party on deck, and slipped ashore by himself. He walked a few blocks from the pier and the milling crowd, until he could hail a passing taxi.

By doing this, he reached the Hotel Maamura Palace several minutes ahead of the others. He checked in quickly, tipped a bellman to take his bag to his room, and hit the streets again. At a magazine kiosk, he purchased a detailed street map of Alexandria.

The address he had been given by Tomopoles in Rhodes

was deep in the old quarter of the city, light-years away from the high-rise buildings of glass and steel.

Now he shunned cabs and walked instead, always keeping an eye over his shoulder. It was nearly an hour before he found the street he sought. It was scarcely more than a rancid-smelling alley with windowless walls pierced by single, narrow doorways. He passed few pedestrians, and none of them gave him more than a glance, intent as they were to reach their homes and their evening meals. The only sign of life was an occasional stall-like shop presided over by an indifferent and lethargic clerk.

The deeper Carter went, the more the sounds of city traffic faded into the background like sounds in a dream.

At last he found the correct number, and entered through an arched door into a musty lobby. A wall directory listed several companies, all but one in Arabic.

Wines of the World was in French and the office was on the third floor.

Carter ascended a narrow stairway between hot stone walls, lit by a single bulb on each landing. It was difficult to believe that any business was conducted in the building, or, for that matter, that there was any life at all. Behind each door he passed it was as quiet as a mummy's tomb.

On the third floor he went down a wide corridor until he found the right door and knocked. The peephole slid aside, closed, and the door opened.

"Welcome to Egypt," said Mahmoud Bey as Carter slipped by him into an office that could have been the clone of the Greek's on Rhodes.

The Egyptian checked the hall, and closed and locked the door. Then, jamming a small cigar between his teeth, he moved behind the paper-strewn desk and sat. Carter took a cracked leather chair opposite, and shook his head at the offer of a cigar.

"How was the boat ride?"

"Illuminating on some fronts, a little boring on others."
Carter told Bey about the Ortega seduction that had turned
into an interrogation.

Bey nodded. "We have word that they are checking you
out."

Carter frowned. "Does that mean that Ortega is more
than just a writer? Is she mixed up with Bachman?"

"Tal would have to fill you in on that, but, yes, she has
known Bachman before. In fact, they have met on several
social occasions in Europe."

Carter lit a cigarette and inhaled deeply. "This damned
thing could get very sticky before it's over. Talk to me
about the newlyweds."

Bey riffled some notes. "Clothilde Irion was born in
Marseille. Nothing on her parents. She was an orphan, raised
in a convent school. She popped up in Paris about two years
ago. She hasn't made many friends, and there aren't too
many people with information on her."

"Is she really a singer?"

"Of sorts," Bey said with a shrug. "Mostly in small
boites, the sing-for-your-supper kind of place."

Carter's frown deepened. "That could hardly make her a
top-drawer chanteuse who could play a club as international
as the Aladdin's Lamp in Cairo."

"Hardly. Tal's people did some nosing around in Paris.
About a year ago, Clothilde was arrested in a student demonstration in front of the American embassy."

"What kind of demonstration?"

"Against your bombing of Libya."

"That's something," Carter said. "At least that gives us
an inkling of her political views. Any connection to Bachman?"

"None that we could dig up. One interesting thing,

though. It seems that Maruja Ortega introduced Clothilde to her future husband.''

"So that would give us a hard connection between Boudia and Ortega. What about him?"

"Now, that's a different tale," Bey replied. "A *very* different tale."

"How so?"

"He doesn't exist."

"I beg your pardon?"

"There is no Zayak Boudia. His French passport is a phony. No passport was ever issued in that name. Also, French immigration keeps excellent files on anyone coming into the country from Beirut, Lebanon. For that matter, on *anyone* coming in from any Middle Eastern country. No Zayak Boudia."

"Very interesting," Carter growled. "Could Tal's informants get anything on him out of Lebanon?"

The other man sighed. "Be serious, Nick. With the mess there now, no one can get anything out of Beirut. If there were records, they have probably been destroyed. But they are still trying. Are you sure he's Lebanese?"

"No, not sure. That's what Ortega told Ruth. Somehow I have a gut feeling that the two of them—Zayak in particular—are integral to this whole thing. They'll be staying at Shepheard's in Cairo. I'll see what I can come up with there. Anything on their visas?"

Here Bey smiled. "There we found a little light. They were rushed through by a high official in the office of immigration. We're doing a personal background on him, and we have surveillance. His name is Hadi Azia."

Bells clanged in Carter's brain. He quickly told Bey about the young tourist authority official who had interrogated him on the *Solaris*. He had barely finished before Bey was reaching for the telephone.

After five minutes of staccato chatter, he hung up. "Omar and Hadi Azia are brothers. We'll get into them deeper."

"Could Bachman have gotten to high officials in your government?"

Bey's face took on a pained expression. "Sadly, yes. But there is greed in everyone, even devout Muslims."

"Speaking of Muslims, what's the latest on our Sons of Islam migration?"

"Actually, quite a bit. As Tomopoles told you, they all seem to be heading for ports along the Red Sea." Here Bey paused and turned a map of the Middle East around on the desk. "We've picked out four individuals to concentrate on, and trailed them from four different directions to here."

"Saudi Arabia?"

Bey nodded. "The port city of Jidda, to be exact."

"Isn't that odd?"

"Not really. It's the ninth month of our Moslem lunar calendar, Ramadan."

"So?"

"So, in the tenth month, which begins next week, the season of the hajj begins."

"The annual pilgrimage to Mecca," Carter mused.

"Right. A great many Moslems are too poor all their lives to make the pilgrimage. A lot of these boys are no different. If Bachman is upping their paychecks, they might figure this is the time to do their religious duty before the pay is cut off."

Carter sat for several minutes, smoking and studying the map. He was about to ask some questions, when the telephone jangled. Bey answered it, grunted a few times, and stood.

"Our place of contact is the Pension El Sabat in Cairo. It's run by a Madame Genevieve Corot. She's French, but she's been working for us for quite some time."

"Can I take this?"

"Of course." As Carter folded the map, Bey wrote a number on a pad. "Just call this number when you want a meet. Tell the person answering that you need a prescription."

"Will do."

The two men shook hands and Carter left. He zigzagged through the teeming city by back alleys. Near the hotel, he popped into a bookstore that was about to close for the night.

"Do you have an English-language section?"

"Yes, sir, right this way."

"Specifically on religion, Islam . . . in English."

It was an odd request, but the pretty young clerk managed to find him four thin volumes. He paid and walked the four remaining blocks to the hotel. From the lobby he called Ruth Melzer's room and got no answer.

Just as he stepped from the phone booth and headed for the dining room, he thought he saw Zayak Boudia jump into an elevator.

Avoids me like the plague, Carter thought, and entered the dining room. He was mulling over the menu and finishing his first drink, when Clothilde Irion Boudia entered. By that hour the room had mostly emptied. Her eyes drifted around the tables, met Carter's, and got nervous. She looked like a fawn lost in the forest. Carter stood.

"Madame Boudia, would you care to join me?"

"Uh, yes . . . thank you. Everyone else has already dined."

Carter escorted her back to the table and seated her. He couldn't help but notice that she was as nervous as a cat. He also couldn't help but notice that she had shed the shapeless black thing she had worn on the ship. In its place was a soft blue sheath, low-cut, with a short jacket.

For the first time since he had met her, she was wearing something that didn't hide what turned out to be a quite attractive figure. Even her hair had a different look, and her face had grown younger and more attractive with makeup.

Carter ordered for both of them and poured the wine.

The talk was idle chitchat until Carter said, "Tell me, Clothilde, you seemed so nervous on the ship, and now here. Is something wrong?"

"Wrong?" she laughed—a high, nervous laugh—and her eyes floated around the room. "All these people are so beautiful . . ."

"Pardon me," Carter chuckled, "but I think you are by far the prettiest woman in the room."

"Oh, I don't mean it that way. I mean, their clothes and the way they wear them. And the way they chatter so confidently, and their jewels. Dear God, look at that woman."

Carter looked. She was a statuesque woman of about fifty in a beaded green dress, and her manicure, makeup, and hairdo had probably cost a hundred and fifty dollars that morning. And the jewelry on her wrist and fingers and at her throat wasn't paste.

"Do the rich make you uneasy?"

"Yes, a little. Not because of envy or disapproval. I dream of myself someday being gay and witty. It's just that, right now, I don't belong here."

"But you will, someday?"

"Oh, yes, someday."

The food came, and try as he might Carter could not get her to open up again.

"Where did you meet Maruja Ortega?" he asked.

"At a party in Paris."

"Do you think singing in Cairo will help your career?"

A shrug.

"Do you feel uncomfortable with me?"

"No."

And that was that.

Over brandy, he offered her a cigarette. "No, I have my own." She fished in her bag. "Oh, dear, I forgot, I'm out. I meant to get some in the lobby . . ."

"Have one of mine."

More idle chatter, but she was pushing her nervousness out of sight now and replacing it with what Carter read as determination. And the determination seemed to be in the form of picking his brains. It wasn't as skillfully done as Maruja Ortega's questioning on the *Solaris*, and it was much more obvious.

He countered all her questions the same way, and eventually called for the check.

In the lobby, he remembered. "What is your brand?"

He got two packs from the machine and slipped them into his pocket while he got his key from the desk.

In the elevator, Clothilde moved very close to him and her breathing started to come in little nervous gasps.

"My husband says that you are a very dangerous man."

"Oh?"

"You are also . . . very attractive. Does that sound forward?"

"Not a bit."

"Zayak has gone out . . . drinking. He does that often."

She unsnapped her handbag and fished for a lipstick and mirror. She looked awkward. In the midst of applying her lipstick, she stopped and the color came back to her face. Almost violently she shoved the items back into the bag and snapped it shut.

"I want you to . . . like me . . ." she whispered as the elevator door opened.

"That would be easy to do," Carter said, taking her arm as they walked down the hall.

He stopped by his own door and fished the key from his

pocket. She was as transparent as a freshly scrubbed window pane, but he hadn't yet decided how to play it.

She made the decision. "I wonder, could I have a nightcap with you? I really don't want to go back to an empty room."

"Of course."

In the room, Carter grabbed the ice bucket and went down the hall. He left the door open a crack. When he returned, Clothilde was leafing through the books he had just purchased. When she heard him, she dropped them and whirled, forcing her lips into a wide smile.

"Just thought I'd learn a little bit about the country," he said.

"Y-yes," she stammered, "that's what I should do, too."

Again she was like a skittish kitten, but she moved to the mini-bar where he fixed the drinks. When he turned, her arms slid up around his neck.

"You said you found me attractive . . ."

She had slid the jacket off. The dress beneath it was strapless, and the soft mounds of her breasts rose above it with her breathing.

Carter set the drinks down and took her in his arms. Her body was as stiff as a board when he kissed her, and she was trembling violently. She was trying desperately to be seductive, but she wasn't getting past the schoolgirl stage.

"I think, Clothilde, that you should go to your own room now."

"What? But don't you—"

He slid the jacket over her shoulders, shoved her purse in her hands, and hustled her to the door.

"But you said you found me—"

"Very young and very attractive. Good night, Clothilde."

He closed the door on her startled face and moved across the room to the phone.

"Yes, this is Dietrich. I'm in the Ortega party. Would

you ring Seven-oh-one, the Boudia's room, please?''

"That's Seven-twelve, sir. One moment . . .''

"Oh, never mind, they just walked into my room.''

He hung up and swallowed the scotch he had already poured. Then he rescued the packs of cigarettes from his coat pocket and hit the stairs. On the seventh floor he went down the line to 712, and glued his ear to the door.

He was about to knock, the cigarettes his excuse, when he didn't have to.

He could hear both their voices through the thin door.

''. . .what do you mean, he kicked you out?''

"He did, I swear it! I practically begged him—''

Suddenly there was a loud crack that could have only been a hand on a face. It was followed by a whimper.

"What about the books? You said . . .'' The rest of it—and the reply—couldn't be heard.

Carter could hear him beat her further, and then Zayak's voice was near him in the hallway where the telephone would be.

"Your little girl friend couldn't handle it . . . no, she couldn't even get him into bed . . . how could she give him the tablet, she wasn't in his room long enough . . . damn little, something about books on Islam. A lot of good that does us . . . I don't care, you've read the file on him. I tell you, he and the woman, Melzer, know something . . . I think they want a payoff of some kind . . . . All right, we'll discuss it in the morning.''

Carter had heard enough. He returned to his room, discarding the two packs of cigarettes in a trash bin.

ELEVEN

Carter stood on the steps of the hotel and watched the little party cross to the waiting Rolls. Maruja Ortega entered first, then Ruth. As Zayak Boudia handed his wife into the car, he turned and gave Carter a last, hard look.

The whole thing had been sloppily engineered, even to keeping Ruth and Carter apart that morning. She had managed to slip a note into his hand at the desk:

> *Sorry, couldn't get to your room last night. Couldn't even get away to call. Ortega had me up until dawn dictating stupid research on Bachman. Nothing that couldn't have waited until today, but she had to do it last night. Talk to you at Shepheard's.*

Carter knew why the dictation couldn't wait. Maruja Ortega couldn't very well have had Ruth walk into his room while Zayak was searching it, or asking him questions while Carter was full of scopolamine.

The chauffeur slid the Rolls into gear and it glided across the square and was lost in a narrow street to the south. On the far side of the square, above the roofs of the modern apartment buildings, a minaret stood bold against the blue sky. From somewhere in its depths a loudspeaker blared, calling the faithful to morning prayer.

"Allahu Akbar! Allahu Akbar!" Carter translated in his mind: God is most great! God is most great!

Nearby, a beggar spread his rug on the sidewak and faced Mecca.

Carter returned to the desk and checked out.

"Here are your tickets for the Cairo express. Would you care to have us check your bag straight through, sir?"

"No, I'll carry it."

He headed back through the maze of the lobby toward the street. A man in a shiny dark business suit cleared his throat and sent a rustling sound through potted palms as he hefted himself from a wicker chair. The Killmaster sensed that he had fallen in step behind him.

He was at Carter's shoulder when they reached the revolving doors. The Luger was in Carter's bag, but he was about to squeeze out Hugo when the man spoke, practically in his ear.

"Tal, Mr. Carter, Tal. Walk to the corner cabstand. Take your taxi to the train station from there."

The man went on through the revolving doors. Carter waited a few beats and went through himself. He turned right, walked a block, and got into the solo cab at the stand. Without waiting for an order the driver dropped his flag and sped away.

The moment he hit the main stream of traffic, he started talking without looking around.

"We got a picture of Zayak Boudia this morning in the hotel lobby. They already have it in Tel Aviv. They are doing the same with some prints we took off his coffee cup."

"Fine," Carter replied. "Can you pass something else off for me?"

"That's what I'm for."

"I want a further check on Maruja Ortega's and Clothilde Irion's backgrounds. This time I want their sex lives dug into."

"Sex lives, you said?"

"Sex lives."

"I'll tell them. Here's the station."

He took off without payment.

The Cairo express slid through the suburbs of Alexandria out toward the green expanse of the delta. Because of the wide-gauge rails, the cars were more spacious than those in Europe. In some ways they were also more opulent, with gilt paneling and soft pile carpets.

Carter settled into his first-class compartment, breathing a sigh of relief that he had it to himself. That sigh turned into a growl when the door opened and a middle-aged British couple moved in. He was just about to remove the books and the map from his bag.

"I say, don't let us disturb you. I'm an academic myself, Cambridge, actually. Leighton Forbes. My wife Melissa."

"Happy to meet you," Carter said, using thickly accented English. "Bruno Dietrich."

The birdlike woman perched on the edge of the seat while her husband took the window side.

"Good time to travel down here, you know. Ramadan, and all that. Gives one the real flavor. Oh, I see you're boning up on Islam. Ask me a few questions if you like. You see, Middle Eastern religions are my specialty."

Carter's eyes swiveled up. He saw no guile in either face, only wary smiles.

"Oh, really?" he said.

Carter gazed out the window and let his mind gestate as the scenery rolled past. In the distance he saw a white sail.

It seemed to be gliding through a cotton field, but it was actually on the Nile. Nearer, a dromedary stood rigid near an ancient water wheel.

The learned professor and his petite wife had departed for the dining car ten minutes before. It had been nearly an hour since they had entered the compartment, and in that time the Killmaster had gotten a sketchy but enlightening education in Islam and a brief history lesson.

Allah had said to Abraham, who later revealed to the Prophet Muhammad: "And proclaim unto mankind a pilgrimage." And so, for the last thirteen centuries, the hajj—or annual pilgrimage to Mecca—had been observed.

Now up to four million Moslems a year visited the mosque in the Holy City to worship at its centerpiece, the Kaaba.

Ramadan is the ninth month of the Moslem lunar calendar. Since the Moslem calendar is only 354 days, all seasons advance eleven days each year. The hajj, or pilgrimage, begins after Ramadan in the tenth month.

There were now five days left in Ramadan, six days until the pilgrimage began.

The professor had gone through each stage of the pilgrims' usual fourteen-day stay in or near the Holy City. Upon entering Mecca—which only Moslems can do—they make their greeting to the Kaaba by circling the sacred stone seven times. This done, they move to the village of Mina and the Mount of Mercy, where Muhammad delivered his final sermon from the back of a camel. From there they go to the Plain of Arafat to perform the "standing." This entails standing in the hot sun on the barren plain from noon to sundown in prayer. This done, the pilgrims head back to Mecca with a halt for a night at Muzdalifah, where the rite of stoning the three pillars of Satan is performed.

Carter absorbed all of this, but the real flowering of his

initial hunch came from something far more pragmatic than the hajj itself.

"The Saudis, you know, have recognized the problems of such a huge gathering."

"In what way?" Carter had asked.

"Once, with so many people congregated together, there was a high mortality rate. There were epidemics of smallpox, cholera, and malaria. Much of that has been done away with. Even the tent cities have diminished with the construction of hotels. The more affluent pilgrims can live in comfort in the Mecca Inter-Continental Hotel. Of course, that has brought its own problems."

"You mean, modernizing the hajj?"

"Yes. The purists want to return to the ascetic traditions, do away with airports at Jidda that make the access easier to Mecca, and the hotels that make the stay less arduous. A case in point was the takeover of the mosque in 1979."

Carter remembered. On the morning of November 20 of that year, 350 armed men broke into the Haram, the mosque that encloses the Kaaba. They demanded that one of their people be declared the Mahdi, the Messiah that a few Moslem sects prophesy. The ulema, the religious authority, rejected their demands. That started a siege.

The Moslem world was up in arms to think that any group would desecrate the holy shrine.

Eventually, the mosque was retaken and tempers were cooled when sixty-three of the rebels were beheaded.

But the fact remained: someone had tried.

Now Carter took the penciled map of the Mecca area that the professor had made, and studied it carefully. Then he shifted his concentration to the map of the Middle East.

The Drogo tribesman had said that the Israeli fighter-bomber had come in from the Mediterranean Sea over Tobruk, Libya. It had been moving fast and low, and it had headed due south into the desert.

Carter began to theorize.

What if the plane hadn't landed in Libya? What if it had continued on into the deep Sahara of the Sudan? There were thousands of square miles of barren desert where it could be hidden. And it would be on a direct east-west line, with a flight time of one hour.

Suddenly Carter's hands shook. The ash jiggled off his cigarette and the map rattled.

He had it.

The crazy bastards were going to bomb Mecca.

Shepheard's was in the Garden City section of Cairo, right on the Nile. The original hotel had stood near Opera Square, but it was one of the casualties of the 1952 revolution when Nasser and company ousted King Farouk. It had been burned to the ground by the rioting mobs.

When it was rebuilt in 1956, they had tried to re-create the mood of Moorish and Victorian architecture, and failed. But of all the hotels in Cairo it still maintained the charm of a bygone era.

Carter checked in and, without going to his room, hit one of the lobby phones that had a direct line. He dialed the number Bey had given him in Alexandria, and it was picked up before the first ring ended.

"Asallah Drugs."

"Tal," Carter said. "I find that I am in need of a prescription right away."

"A second, please . . . " Carter lit a cigarette and checked out the lobby while he waited to see if anyone was checking him out. "Are you there?"

"Yes."

"One hour."

The line went dead, and Carter went to the magazine kiosk for a map of Cairo. When he had located the area, he hit the streets. He cabbed to within a mile of the Pension El Sabat, and dived into narrow side streets where anyone following him would have one hell of a hard time.

The Pension El Sabat was depressing, one step above a flophouse. In the small, evil-smelling lobby, an ancient redheaded woman sat at the desk under a harsh light.

"Madame Genevieve Corot?"

"*Non*. I am her sister."

"I would like to see Madame Genevieve."

"A name?"

"Tal."

"Number Twenty-eight, second floor."

Carter walked up a flight of ill-lighted stairs into a long, narrow hall where one yellowish bulb burned eerily over the exit door at the far end. He used his lighter to find room 28, and knocked. After a few seconds, the door was opened an inch to reveal part of a woman's face.

"Well?"

"I've come to collect my prescription."

"Come in."

Carter slipped through the door and it was closed quickly behind him. It was a large, two-room apartment, one side a bedroom, the room where he stood an office. Mahmoud Bey rose from a sofa as Carter entered.

"I didn't expect to hear from you for at least another twenty-four hours."

"I think I've figured it out," Carter growled, and glanced at the woman.

"I'll be down at the desk if you need me," she said, and left the room.

The instant the door closed behind her, Carter spread out the map and the notes he had taken on a low table between the couch and a chair.

"You've got the location of the plane?"

"No, but I think I know why they wanted it. Mahmoud, how many times have you made the pilgrimage to Mecca?"

The Egyptian chuckled. "Never. I always plan to, of course. It's a Moslem's duty. But I haven't yet."

"Right," Carter said. "A lot of Moslems haven't. Now, suddenly, a large contingent of the Sons of Islam brotherhood decides that this year is the time to take their pilgrimage. I don't think they are making their hajj at all. I think they are going to Mecca to be the first inciters or on-site propagandists for a holy war."

"What are you getting at?" Bey said.

"I'm getting at this," Carter replied, his voice dropping into a low monotone. "It's a piece of addition. Our Sons of Islam are the most fanatical of all the terrorist groups and sects. They now have a wealthy and powerful ally in a devoted anti-Semite, Herr Otto Bachman. They have an Israeli airplane loaded with rockets and bombs . . ."

"Nick, you can't be serious." Mahmoud Bey's usually swarthy complexion lost about two shades of color.

"I'm deadly serious," Carter growled. "The bastards are going to bomb the holy shrine with an Israeli plane. How better to unite all the Arab peoples and start one hell of a holy war to end all wars?"

"But these men, the Sons of Islam followers, they're Moslems themselves. They would never take part in such a sacrilege."

"They might," Carter said, "if the mosque itself is not hit. What if they hit the Inter-Continental Hotel, here at Mecca, as well as the hotels in Mina, and the tent cities on the plain?"

"It's crazy!"

"You bet your ass it's crazy, and I think these people are crazy enough to do it. The mosque was taken once, remember, in 1979? That was by Moslems, and all hell broke loose. Can you imagine three million witnesses to an Israeli plane dropping bombs and rockets on them? It won't matter that the Kaaba isn't hit. As far as all those people on the ground are concerned, the intent is there—they just missed!'

"But Mecca itself is attacked?"

"Exactly. All the Arab leaders will have to mobilize against Israel. If they don't, they'll have revolt on their hands."

Mahmoud Bey ran the tip of his thumb over Mecca on the map until his eyes were glassy. "All they need is a trained pilot."

"That's right," Carter said. "Now, here's—"

"And they've got him."

"What?"

"Zayak Boudia. Tel Aviv couldn't come up with anything on him, but your own Air Force did. He's Iranian. His real name is Asvial Houbourak. He was one of the last group of pilots trained in your country under the Shah. He graduated with the highest marks in his class."

"Jesus," Carter groaned, "it was right in front of me and I didn't see it."

Suddenly Bey bolted to his feet. "The responsibility is too great. I've got to inform the Saudis."

"No, not yet," Carter said. "An alert like that would just tip off Bachman. No telling what he would do . . . move his timetable up, pick a different target, anything. No, we've got five days; let's use them. In Alexandria, I asked your cab driver for a rundown—"

"Right here."

Carter took the single sheet of paper and scanned it quickly. Nothing concrete on Clothilde, but a lot on Maruja Ortega.

"Ortega's a lesbian?"

Bey shrugged. "Not wholeheartedly, evidently, but according to that, she leans toward young ladies."

"I think I know where Clothilde fits now. Does that phone have a direct outside line?"

"Yes."

Carter dialed Shepheard's and asked for the Boudias' room.

"There is no answer, sir."

"Thank you. This is Bruno Dietrich. Any messages?"

"Yes, one, Herr Dietrich. Should I read it to you?"

"Yes, please."

" 'Bruno, I must see you tonight. Urgent that we discuss important matter. I'm staying in the guesthouse of Bachman's villa. Come at midnight, but don't use the main gate. There is a wooden door in the rear wall off of the stable grounds. It will be open. Maruja.' That is the message, sir."

"Thank you." Carter hung up and turned to Bey with a satisfied smile on his face.

"Something? You look as though you have just bartered three sick camels for the price of six healthy ones."

Carter shrugged. "Maybe I have, maybe I haven't. But one thing is for sure—I've got them thinking. Ortega wants to see me in her private quarters at Bachman's villa."

Carter thought the other man would be elated. Instead, Bey was frowning and worrying the end of his cigar until it shredded in his teeth.

"Do you think it wise, my friend, to approach the lioness in her own den at this time?"

"Do you have a better suggestion?"

"No," Bey replied with a shrug. "But if they think you are an adventurer out for gain from their efforts . . ."

"That's a reasonable risk to take," Carter said, pulling the map of Cairo from his jacket. "Draw me directions on this to Bachman's villa . . . and I'll need a very unofficial-looking car for the night."

Mahmoud Bey drew lines with arrows on the map and handed it back to Carter. "Should we pick up Zayak Boudia?"

"God, no. That's all we need to do, alert them that we know as much as we do. Put some people on him, but tell them whatever they do, don't alert him. If we've got them off the track and they think I'm a free-lancer looking for a quick mark, that's all the better."

"We should make arrangements for you and the woman to pull out if there are problems."

"Fair enough," Carter said.

Bey scribbled on a piece of paper. "This is the address of a Nubian who tracks the Bedouin smugglers for us in the south. It is in the old city, on Darb el Ahmar . . . the Red Alley."

Carter memorized those directions and handed the paper back. "Let's hope I won't need it."

TWELVE

Ruth Melzer, dressed in black flowing robes from her head to her toes, darted through the tiny streets with Clothilde at her heels. It had already been quite an evening, and, from the looks of it, the night to come would be even more rewarding.

Zayak and Clothilde Boudia had dined at the villa with Bachman, Maruja, and herself. Immediately after the meal, Boudia and Bachman had disappeared into the German's study. Maruja had pleaded a headache and gone to her quarters.

Almost the instant they were alone, Clothilde had broken down.

"Late this afternoon, a man came to our rooms at the hotel. He said he was with the government and . . . and he knows . . ."

"Knows what, Clothilde?"

"He knows that my marriage is a sham, that I was being used to get Zayak into Egypt and safely back out."

"Is that true, Clothilde?" Ruth had asked.

"Yes . . ." Then the tears came and it all poured out.

Maruja Ortega had befriended Clothilde in Paris. They

had become lovers. Clothilde was given an apartment, clothes, spending money, and promises from the older woman that one day soon she would have a boost in her career.

Then, a few weeks earlier, she was asked to do this little thing as a favor to Maruja. She would be given a chance to sing at the Aladdin's Lamp in Cairo. In return, she must go through this mock wedding with Zayak Boudia.

"But why, Clothilde? Why did they need you to get Zayak into the country?"

"I don't know," the younger girl had sobbed. "I was never told. And then last night Zayak made me try and seduce your friend . . ."

"Bruno Dietrich?"

"Yes. He wanted me to put a pill in his drink."

A chill had run up Ruth's spine. "Did you do it?"

"No, I couldn't," Clothilde had whimpered, her whole body shaking. "Zayak was very angry. He beat me. When the man came this afternoon, he knew all of this. He said I could be in a great deal of trouble, but he could help me. He said that you could be trusted, that I could confide in you."

"Clothilde, what was the man's name?"

"Mahmoud Bey. He said that you would help me slip away from the villa tonight. And then he would get me out of the country and safely back to France before I got in more trouble."

"Where are you to meet him?"

"A small hotel in the old quarter near the Horn, called the Golden Crescent." Her large eyes had looked pleadingly at the other woman. "Will you take me there, Ruth? We are to come in native dress."

"Yes, yes, I will."

How clever of Bachman to keep her and Carter separated,

Ruth thought. It was impossible to talk freely on the phone to the hotel, or for Carter to call her. If Bey had contacted her through Clothilde, everything must be opening up and this was a signal to get away.

She had rifled the servants' quarters for native dress, and a half hour later they had walked out the gates together. From a pay phone she had called Carter. He was not in his room and he had left no message.

They had found a taxi into the city and now, through the gauzy mask of her black veil, she was trying to find the Golden Crescent.

"Ruth, there, on the corner!" Clothilde suddenly cried.

It was a small hotel whose façade was hung with iron balconies and peeling gingerbread. Together they entered the lobby. It was dim and had an unpleasant odor, like the interior of a musty, damp cave.

There was a little Turk, the fez on his head bobbing nervously as he watched them approach the desk.

"We were told to arrive at eleven," Ruth said in Arabic.

"Yes, follow me."

They were led down a dirty hallway, up some steps, and into a room.

"Wait here one minute," the Turk said, and left.

Clothilde sank into the room's only chair while Ruth looked around. The room was in the rear of the hotel. The single window opened onto a dark alley. Opposite was the blank wall of the neighboring building.

The room itself showed no signs of occupancy. There was not a book or a scrap of paper anywhere. The open closet door revealed unused hangers.

The silence was oppressive, and for the first time since leaving the villa, Ruth began to have doubts. For reassurance, she moved her hand to the small of her back to touch the Beretta held fast in the belt of her slacks.

There was a sound in the hall. Ruth raised her veil for better vision, and moved across the room to place herself flat against the wall beside the door.

"What is it?" Clothilde asked, a quiver in her voice.

"Shhh!"

The knob turned gently, then the door swung in and a man entered. It wasn't Mahmoud Bey.

Ruth kicked the door closed and shoved the muzzle of the Beretta into the small of his back. "Put your hands on your head and turn around very slowly."

He did.

"You!"

"I'm flattered and glad that you remember me from the *Solaris*, Fräulein Melzer," said Omar Azia.

"Clothilde, is this the man who came to your hotel room?"

"No, no, it isn't," the girl replied, wide-eyed.

"Calm yourself," he said, never taking his eyes from the Beretta in Ruth's hand. "I have been working with Mahmoud Bey for the past few days. His office asked for my help in the matter of the Boudia visas."

"Where is Bey?"

"He is with Herr Dietrich. They will be here shortly. I am to debrief you and assimilate what we have all learned before they arrive. Shall we sit?"

"I'm all right where I am," Ruth replied curtly.

Azia shrugged and lit a cigarette. Ruth noticed that his hands weren't too steady. She tried to catch his eyes but they were darting everywhere.

"These walls have no ears," he said. "We can talk. We now have irrefutable proof that there is an Israeli plane. We still do not know where the plane is or what is to be done with it. Have you gleaned anything at the villa?"

Ruth was torn. It was conceivable that Bey had enlisted

Omar Azia's help. But what if he hadn't?

Dammit! Why couldn't I have gotten in touch with Carter!

"I think I'll wait for Bey to arrive."

Azia shrugged. He dropped the cigarette on the carpet and ground it out with his heel. "As you wish. But time is of the essence. Even now, Bachman and the pilot are leaving the villa and going to the German's houseboat on the Nile . . ."

"The pilot?"

Azia smiled. "You see, we have been working. Her husband, Zayak Boudia," he said, nodding toward Clothilde, "is a highly trained Iranian pilot. We must assume that he has been smuggled into the country to fly the plane . . . but where?"

Ruth sighed and slipped the gun back into her waistband. "I don't know. I've tried to listen in on telephone conversations, and I've gone through the papers in Bachman's desk. Nothing."

Suddenly Azia snapped out a phrase in Arabic. The door behind Ruth opened. Ruth wheeled, reaching for the Beretta. Her hand stopped in mid-movement. The man coming through the door had a silenced revolver, the muzzle inches from her face.

"Ruth!" Clothilde cried, "that's the man who came to my hotel room!"

"Good evening, Fräulein Melzer. I am Omar's brother. My name is Hadi Azia."

Carter drove south along the Nile. It was just a little after ten o'clock when he reached the affluent suburb of Cairo called Maadi. It was beautiful, with wide, tree-lined streets and large old houses. He was through it in minutes and on the Helwan Highway.

Two miles further on, he spotted the turnoff and headed

directly for the Nile. It wasn't difficult to spot Bachman's villa. It was huge, on a rise above the river. There was a high stone wall surrounding the grounds on three sides, the river itself being the fourth.

He drove about a mile past the grounds, and left the car in a grove of date palms. Then he climbed to higher ground and had a look-see.

In the rear of the villa, gardens led down to the river and a dock. Moored to the dock was a huge houseboat lit up like a Christmas tree.

Directly below him and going all the way to the wall were stables, pastures, and a large riding ring. Just inside the wall, he spotted the guest cottage. It looked to be about the size of a normal house, perhaps seven or eight rooms, with a large veranda facing the villa.

The main gate in the front wall was well lit, and Carter spotted two gatekeepers. Neither of them appeared armed, but he knew that meant nothing.

He jogged until he hit a wooden fence near the river, and went through. He moved like a shadow through the riding ring and then the stable area. There was an open, moonlit area of about a hundred yards.

He gathered himself and charged across it, not stopping until he was in the shadow of the wall. He inched along the wall until he found the recess and then, by feel, the wooden door.

He looked at the illuminated dial of his watch. It was almost eleven. He would be exactly one hour early.

The door opened easily, and Carter slid through into a garden. Ten long strides took him to the bungalow. He ducked under a scarlet awning leading into the garden from the rear veranda, and edged toward a pair of glass doors, peering cautiously through the panes.

Inside was as exquisite sitting room, as extravagantly

decorated as a luxurious townhouse, all in blues, eggshell, and gold.

There was no sound other than faint music from a radio turned low.

He moved fast through the glass doors and closed them quietly behind him. As he moved across the room, he took the Luger from his ankle holster and flipped off the safety.

He found himself in a small foyer. On the opposite side, an arched doorway led into a mirror-lined dining room where a long table sparkled with linen and silver. In the center of the foyer was a gilt railing and steps leading downward. He descended quickly, holding the Luger ready.

It was a long hall with three paneled doors. The music emanated from behind the second door. Taking a deep breath, he reached for the knob, pushed inward, stepped across the threshold, and shut it softly behind him.

It was a small but elegantly appointed sitting room. Light streamed through a door to the left. Carter stood still, listening. From somewhere came the sound of splashing water.

The scent of expensive perfume and soap hung in the air. Carter smiled. He was pretty sure he had chosen the right door. Quietly, he moved toward the light.

It was a fantastic bedroom, a harem chamber right out of some sultan's wildest dream. The walls were draped with red silks, and the centerpiece was a bed that could easily sleep eight. To the left of the bed, through a half-opened door, he saw a woman seated in a black marble bathtub.

Even though her back was to Carter, he knew it was Maruja Ortega. His guess about the remarkable preservation of her body proved accurate when she came up out of the water and stepped from the tub.

He lounged against a doorjamb and enjoyed the view as she reached for a towel and began to pat herself dry. This done, she powdered her body and took the pins from her hair so that it cascaded in luxurious waves to her shoulders.

Carter moved back into the bedroom as she turned. In profile, she shook her hair loose and stretched. The line of her body was breathtaking. Then she turned and came into the bedroom, discarding the towel on the way.

Carter remained silent in the shadow of the great tent of fabric over the bed, watching. She stopped before a mirror and reached for a perfume bottle. She removed the glass stopper and glided it between her breasts. She smiled into the mirror as she drew the stopper down across her stomach. She half closed her eyes and brought her hips forward in a sensual movement that sent shock waves clear across the room.

"Very nice."

Carter came out of the shadows. She wheeled about, her eyes wide with fear. But almost instantly the fear died and was replaced by an expression so primitive in its meaning that not even a eunuch could have missed it.

"In the message, I said midnight."

"I know," Carter replied. "I like to be extra prompt."

She moved forward until the tips of her breasts were nearly touching his chest. "Or extra careful?"

"Both."

She shrugged, and the movement made her breasts dance. "It's just as well. We must talk, eventually. But now we might have time for . . . other things."

"Such as?"

"Finishing what you tried to start the other evening."

"We might," Carter said.

When he made no move to touch her, Maruja moved to a closet and shrugged into a thin negligee. She tied it in the front and turned back to him. It hid nothing and flattered everything.

"You are in danger," she murmured.

"How so?" He followed her lithe movement to a small bar.

"Because of your background, Otto Bachman is afraid that you will commit some crime while you are in Egypt. Since you entered the country as part of my entourage, he is very angry with me. In fact, he has refused to grant me the articles unless I vouch for you."

Carter decided to go along with it. "And what do you want from me?"

"Assurance that you will be a good boy while you are here. Can you give me that?"

He took the drink she offered him and tried to figure her. Could she not know what was coming off? Could Bachman just be using her?

"I think you know, Bruno," she continued, "that my political views coincide with Herr Bachman's. If your past is any indication, we must both agree that you also agree with the Palestinian cause."

"I think you could assume that, yes."

She maneuvered close again, and tugged him down with her to a settee. "One of Herr Bachman's favorite charities is the Palestinians. If you were smart, you would get close to him. He might even find some employment for you in his organization."

Carter crushed out his cigarette. "Is that why you wanted to see me tonight?"

"That . . . and other things."

The Killmaster tried to put it together. Could she not know about Zayak Boudia? Could she believe she was merely doing the "cause" and Bachman a favor?

Her body pressed against his as her arms glided around his neck. "That was why I told you to come at midnight. He will be finished with his meetings then. I would like to introduce you to him."

Over her shoulder, Carter glanced at his watch. "It's eleven-thirty."

"I'm sure we can find something to occupy the time," she purred, stroking the back of his head with her fingertips. She had graceful hands, long and tapering.

Suddenly she was moving, pulling him to his feet. His hands drifted to her waist. Her scent was heady and her warmth through the thin negligee was getting to him.

"Why is tonight so different from the other night in my stateroom?" he growled.

"Mood," she said, panting. "Isn't a woman allowed her moods?"

Carter drew her tightly against him until their two bodies were molded as one from upper chest to knees. Her thighs and hips, when he kissed her, began to thrust against him insistently. Also, he could feel the pressure of her lower belly.

"Mmm, that's nice," she sighed.

He covered her buttocks with his hands and tugged her even closer.

She tore her mouth from his. Her face, normally stern, was now tinted with the pinkness of passion, and she was breathing heavily.

"Let me undress you . . . now," she gasped.

Though his body had risen to the challenge of her flesh, Carter was mentally and spiritually aloof. He regarded her with detachment as she removed his clothing.

Then she found the gun. She unstrapped the holster from his ankle and held it up. "A Luger," she said very calmly. "How many have you killed with this, Bruno Dietrich?"

He took the gun, swept her into his arms, and practically threw her on the bed. He put the Luger on the bedside stand and shucked the rest of his clothing.

She was lying on her back, her lips parted, her breasts

heaving. Her magnificent body was practically glowing through the transparent negligee.

All right, Carter thought, *let's see how far the game goes*.

He gathered his fingers in the negligee at her breasts and shredded it. Then he was on top of her, his hips grinding. His tongue forced an entry through her teeth and began thrusting inside her mouth. One of his hands found a full breast and cruelly squeezed.

It was then that he saw the smile on Maruja's face and the glazed look in her wide eyes. He knew he was hurting her, and he could see that she was loving it.

He dropped between her thighs and entered her savagely. It brought a moan of pleasure from her lips and she responded by digging her long, sharp nails into his back.

If the report given him on her by Mahmoud Bey hadn't enlightened him about Maruja Ortega, what he was seeing now did.

The more he punished her with his body, the wilder she got. Her body was lurching to meet him. She moaned and twisted beneath him like something possessed.

Somewhere in the distance he heard a clock striking.

It was midnight. But as her legs and arms wound about him, he knew they had only just begun.

Otto Bachman watched the monitors with one eye, and kept the other on the clock. Now and then he adjusted the volume to hear each word.

"Damn," he hissed to himself, "one is early and the other is late!"

Then he smiled. Maruja was quick. If she hadn't already proved a hundred times how far she was willing to go, she was proving it now. The man was about to leave. He had sensed it, and so had she.

But she had kept him there with her body.

The telephone beside Bachman rang. "Yes?"

"This is Azia. The two women kept the appointment."

"Well?"

"It is obvious that Fräulein Melzer knows who Mahmoud Bey is. Also, they know of the plane's existence. She let her guard down just long enough for us to learn that."

"And what did she say of Dietrich?"

"Nothing. She tumbled to us before I could probe anything more out of her. But I am positive that they do not know the whereabouts of the plane, and the woman was obviously surprised when I mentioned that Boudia was the pilot."

"Good," Bachman replied. "We might still be able to stay on schedule. You have them there?"

"Yes, drugged, both of them."

"Excellent. Bring them on the river to the houseboat. And make sure you are not seen."

Bachman hung up just as he heard a car on the gravel path in the front. He bolted from his chair and practically ran to the front door. The tall, patrician-looking man with the calm gray eyes and the handsome head of dark hair sprinkled with gray had barely stepped from the car when Bachman reached him.

"You're over an hour late!" the German fumed.

"My dear Bachman, sneaking over the border from Libya to Egypt in the dead of night is not an easy task."

"Yes, yes, I know. Come along. Maruja has him occupied. You can view him on the monitor."

The two men entered the villa and moved down the hall.

"Also, Otto, if your people had been able to get a better photograph of him, this trip would not have been necessary."

Bachman didn't reply, but turned into the study and went directly to the television monitor. The other man stopped at his side, his eyes glistening as he watched the writhing couple on the bed.

"Charming. I see my darling Maruja has lost none of her technique."

"Forget that," Bachman hissed. "Who is he?"

"A moment . . . a moment, Otto. I cannot see his face clearly . . . there."

The couple had rolled away from each other and now lay on their backs.

The man standing beside Bachman smiled. "That, my dear Otto, is not Bruno Dietrich."

"You're sure?"

"Positive. That is an American agent named Nick Carter."

Now it was Bachman's turn to smile. "You are absolutely sure?"

"As sure as my own name is Marcel Isban."

Carter lay for several seconds, breathing heavily. When the telephone rang, he started to rise. She brushed her lips across his and pushed him back down.

"That will be Otto. He is probably ready to see you now. I'll get it." She rolled to her side away from him and picked up the phone. "Yes . . . yes, of course . . . I understand . . . right away." She hung up and eased from the bed. "Get dressed."

Maruja Ortega was once again her old self.

Carter rolled off his side of the bed and walked around to where his clothes littered the floor. He pulled on his shorts and pants, and then reached for the Luger. The moment it was in his hand he noticed the change in weight.

"Looking for this?"

He looked up.

In one hand she dangled the clip from the Luger. Steady,

in her other hand, was a snub-nosed .38 revolver, the hammer already pulled back.

From somewhere outside, Carter heard the roar of a powerful diesel engine and the sound of running feet.

There was one slug in the chamber of the Luger. He knew he could get Ortega, but the sound of the door opening behind him told him that someone would get him before he got his hands on her gun or the clip.

"Well?" Maruja said, not taking her eyes from Carter's.

"He's an American agent. His name is Nick Carter."

The Killmaster turned.

The first man he recognized from the film Hawk had shown him. He had no trouble recognizing the second man as Marcel Isban.

And he was sure Isban had had no trouble recognizing him.

THIRTEEN

Carter wasn't sure if it was the throb of the engine or the rocking of the boat—or both—that brought him out of his stupor.

He opened his eyes, but he didn't move. The stateroom was small but well furnished. There was the usual furniture, and through a small porthole he could see blue sky.

He sensed movement from the other bunk, and rolled his head around.

Ruth Melzer lay on the bunk, her eyes open, staring at the overhead.

"Ruth . . ."

At the sound of his voice she was up, across the space between the beds, and sitting beside him.

"My god, you're alive! Sometimes you were hardly breathing. I thought you were dead!"

"They gave me a hypo. That's the last thing I remember. We're on the houseboat, aren't we?"

"Yes. We've been moving all night, but I don't know which way and I don't know where we are."

Carter closed his eyes and concentrated. "We're going against the current, upstream. I can tell from the way the engine is working."

153

Ruth's brow furrowed in concentration. "The Nile flows out of Egypt and empties into the Med at Alexandria. That means we're going deeper into the country . . . toward Aswan."

Carter nodded and felt his head throb. Slowly, he managed to get up to a sitting position and plant his feet on the deck. He noticed he was fully dressed, including socks and shoes, and the previous night's events washed back over him.

"They drugged me, too," Ruth said.

"At the villa?"

"No." She turned away and a flush crept up her cheeks. "I screwed up, walked right into one."

Carter managed a mirthless chuckle. "Don't worry about it; so did I. Tell me about yours first."

Ruth was quick, no nonsense. She gave him the salient facts and didn't try to embellish them to make herself look good. Carter didn't speak until she paused.

"You think Clothilde is faking it?" he asked, patting his pockets for cigarettes.

She noticed the movement. "Your cigarettes and the rest of your things are there on the table. But don't bother. They took both of our lighters and a book of matches I had in my purse."

"Figures. Well?"

"Clothilde? No, she wasn't faking it. She was scared out of her head. They drugged her along with me."

"Where is she now?"

"I came awake just for a moment when they were carrying us from the car. They took her to the villa when they brought me to the houseboat."

Carter nodded. "That stands to reason. Zayak Boudia will do his little deed, then he'll probably crash the plane in the desert at some prearranged spot after he's parachuted out. He'll be picked up, brought back to Cairo, and he and his bride will waltz out of the country. Also, unless I miss my guess, little Clothilde will meet with a fatal accident back in Paris . . . or maybe even before she gets there.''

''Your turn, Nick. Just what is Boudia's 'little deed,' as you call it?''

''Zayak is going to fly out of the Sudan over the Red Sea. He'll probably made a wide turn, under radar, north of Jidda, and come in from the north.''

''To where?''

''To Mecca, Ruth. They're going to bomb Mecca with an Israeli Phantom during the first week of the holy pilgrimage.''

Dusk had fallen. No one had come to the stateroom, and the sounds of the river other than the houseboat had faded.

''Where do you think we're going?'' Ruth asked, her face tense.

''Eventually, to the plane.''

''Surely they won't take us all the way to the plane,'' she replied. ''Why should they?''

Carter glanced at her curled up on the other bed. Her eyes looked strained and there was a sudden gauntness in her face.

The inference in her words was clear. Why should they be taken to the plane? It would be far easier to let the swift waters of the Nile take care of them.

Carter cursed silently. He didn't want her to go to pieces. It wouldn't be like her to crack, but it's hard to say what anyone will do when they get to the bottom line.

''I think they have some reason for bringing us this far. As long as they keep us alive, we've got an out.''

Suddenly a jarring tremor went all through the boat. Then the tremor became a shudder.

''What was that?''

"Reversing the engines. We're docking." Even as Carter spoke they could feel the stern angling to starboard. "Where's your purse?"

"Here." She held it up from the bed beside her.

"Give me your compact."

Carter took it and crossed to the porthole. By the time he had his hand outside and had angled the mirror around to where he could see, the boat had stopped moving. Now the engine was on idle, holding the craft still.

They were tying up to a tall mudbank. He could see two of the crew with lines already on top of the bank. When the lines were secure, the two men picked up rifles and moved out of sight.

From the stern, Carter heard voices, but they were too low to identify. It seemed to be just a low babble of lethargic conversation.

Suddenly there were footsteps outside the hatch. Carter pocketed the compact and waited.

The door opened, and Marcel Isban—tall, cool, confident—stepped into the cabin. He wasn't armed, but the two crewmen behind him were, with machine pistols.

"This is a little out of our line, isn't it, Isban?" Carter hissed.

"You are a tenacious man, Carter, but that has worked in our favor."

"Oh? How so?"

"You'll see, in time."

"Where the hell are we?"

"Just south of Abu Simbel, a few miles from the border of Sudan," Isban replied. "Follow me."

He moved down the passageway, with Carter and Ruth behind and the two crewmen bringing up the rear. They climbed the ladder to the main deck, and came out into the cool night air.

Bachman, Zayak Boudia, and the two Azia brothers had already crossed over the gangway and now stood on top of the mudbank with two more armed crewmen.

Maruja Ortega, in a pair of dark slacks and a light sweater, stood by the rail. When Ruth emerged from the hatch and stepped out on the deck, the older woman's eyes smoldered.

"Did the Americans pay you to spy on me, bitch, or do you work for someone else?"

Ruth glanced at Carter and didn't reply. When she got no answer, Maruja crossed the deck.

"I trusted you," she spat. "For years I trusted you! How many of my friends in that time have you compromised?"

Again, silence.

Maruja's hand on Ruth's face was like the crack of a rifle in the still night. Carter leaped forward, but Isban stepped in front of him. The man's fist was like a rock in Carter's gut. Before the Killmaster could right himself and get air, the fist came up into his face.

Carter's head was snapped back by the smashing blow, hitting the wheelhouse wall with a dull thump. He put his left hand behind him and pushed himself erect. A trickle of blood ran from his split upper lip into his mouth.

He started to speak, and Isban hit him again, a sideways blow with his open palm. Carter rolled his head with the blow and kept his feet. One of the crewmen held his machine pistol trained on Carter's midsection, and there was an evil gleam of gratification in his eyes.

Carter said, "This'll cost you, Isban." His tongue licked out over his bloody lip.

Another blow smashed him between the eyes and sent him staggering back.

Carter planted his feet wide apart, shaking his head slowly to banish the shooting stars.

"I would dearly love to kill you here and now, Carter,"

Isban sneered, "but Otto has found a good use for your body elsewhere."

"Enough!" Bachman called from his perch on the mud-bank. "I don't want him marked up. Send them over!"

Prodded by the crewmen, Carter and Ruth maneuvered the gangway. Atop the mudbank, their wrists were tied with leather thongs.

"Maruja . . . Marcel?" The two replied as one. "Sail on to Kerma. We will meet you there in three days' time."

"Kerma it is," Isban nodded. "May Allah forgive us this small sin for the great victory it will bring us."

Carter and Ruth were pushed ahead of the others down a dusty road toward a truck.

Bachman and one of the ship's crewman got in the front. Everyone else piled into the rear, and a canvas flap was dropped. A match flared and lit two cigarettes in Zayak Boudia's lips. He passed one to Carter.

"The first time you saw me, I thought you recognized me. Did you?"

"Not then," Carter replied. "But when I found out your real name, where you had taken your flight training in the States, and the fact that you are an Iranian . . . then I remembered that I had seen your picture in *The New York Times* years ago."

"Yes," Boudia sighed, drawing deeply on his cigarette so its glow illuminated the beatific smile on his face. "Even then I was destined for greatness."

"I think you, like your boss, are sick."

"Come, come, American Carter, we should be friends. We will soon ride to glory together!"

Carter didn't even want to think what he meant by that.

In between jolts and lurches in the rear of the old truck, Carter and Ruth napped. It was impossible to tell if the

others slept or not. It really made no difference. Their wrists
were tied securely with the leather thongs, and even though
their feet were free they weren't going anywhere. Leaping
from the truck in the middle of the night in the vast Sahara
would be foolhardy.

Dawn, breaking from the east, was announced through
slight cracks in the canvas over the bed of the truck. As
was always the case in the desert, the sun gave immediate
heat.

It was chilly in the truck, so the warmth was welcome
to captor and captive alike. Someone rolled up the rear flap,
and someone else opened two side panels.

Carter pushed himself to a sitting position and gazed out
at the vast emptiness. The drowsiness left him at once.

He figured it was ten to one that sometime during the
night they had passed over a remote part of the frontier.
From the position of the sun, Carter guessed that they were
moving due southwest.

He closed his eyes and concentrated, conjuring up a map.
Only detailed topography charts would show the smallest
village or oasis, and these he wasn't familiar with. They
were passing through rolling, low dunes. That would mean
they were still east of the vast Khabir range. That meant
that before them was only one oasis of any real size, Selima.

Carter didn't doubt that they would pass far to one side
or the other of that.

Suddenly they rolled over a rise and dropped into a huge
wadi. When the ground leveled out at the bottom, the truck
lurched to a stop.

Bachman's face appeared in the side flap. "Everyone
out! This is the halfway point. We will spend the day here!"

The tarp was removed from the truck, and in no time a
makeshift tent was erected. The two crew members from
the boat, now dressed in gray desert robes, worked quickly

and efficiently. In no time a camp was set up and a fire was built.

From a crate on the roof of the cab, a baby goat was led out. Zayak Boudia dispatched the animal with one clean cut of a knife, and minutes later the smell of roasting meat filled the bottom of the wadi.

As the meat cooked it was stripped away in layers and handed around. Only then did Carter realize that he hadn't eaten in nearly twenty-four hours. He attacked the proffered meat with a ravenous appetite, and noticed that Ruth was doing the same. The meat was accompanied by dry, pre-baked pita bread, and washed down with highly sweetened mint tea.

When everyone had eaten his fill, they moved into the makeshift tent to avoid the oncoming heat. Bachman, glass in hand, hunkered down beside Carter.

"You never had a chance to stop us, you know, right from the beginning."

"Is that so?"

"This plan has been in the making for two years. When it is complete, every Moslem in the world will react. They will rise up as one and push the Jews into the sea."

"In theory," Carter said, nodding, "you're probably right."

"Oh, I'm right," the man replied with a smug smile. "And it has gone beyond theory. It is now fact."

"Just what do you get out of this, Bachman?"

The smile was as cold and flat as his eyes. "What do I get? Why, satisfaction, of course."

Boudia walked to where they stood. He carried a small flight bag which he dropped at Carter's feet. "Get up."

The Killmaster did, and the Iranian removed the leather strips from his wrists. This done, he pulled a pair of dark blue flight coveralls from the bag. As he did, Carter noticed that his Luger, the clip still removed, and his stiletto were in the bottom of the bag.

Carter glanced at Bachman. "Thinking about keeping my tools as souvenirs?"

"Quite the opposite," the man snorted. "They will be returned to you, in time. We wouldn't want anything out of the ordinary when you are found."

"Found where?"

"In time, dear Carter, in time."

The man had said enough. Already a germ of an idea was forming in Carter's mind.

"Put these on," Boudia said, pushing the coveralls into Carter's arms.

Carter unfolded them, and as he stepped into them he saw the insignia patch on the shoulder and above the left breast pocket. It was a pair of gold wings inside a silver Star of David.

"A little tight, but it will pass," Boudia said. "Take them off."

"The Phantom," Bachman said, "is a two-seater. Zayak, of course, will fly the plane. You, Carter, will have the privilege of occupying the navigator-gunner's rear seat."

"And when Boudia bails out, I go down with the plane," Carter growled.

"Exactly. Charming, eh? The Israeli pilot somehow escapes into the desert, but the American observer goes down with the aircraft. So not only will Israel be blamed, but the Great Satan, America, as well."

Before Carter could reply, his wrists were rebound and the two men had moved away. Carter moved to the far rear of the tent where Ruth sat dejectedly against one of the poles.

"You saw?"

"Of course I saw. They are going to get away with it, aren't they?"

"Not if I can help it, they're not," Carter replied.

Her eyes blazed. "What the hell are we going to do about it?"

Carter leaned over and brushed his lips across her cheek. "Buck up, old girl. I've still got an ace or two up my sleeve . . . or, rather, leg."

Suddenly she smiled. "You know, you're really not so bad after all. I just hope it's not too late."

"Too late for what?"

"Never mind," she said, lying back and turning away from him. "I'll tell you when the time comes . . . if it comes."

Carter moved in behind behind her and laid his head on the sand.

He did have an idea or two. The only monkey wrench still in the works was . . . what did they plan for her?

The sun goes down fast in the desert. It was just dipping, becoming an orange ball on the western horizon, when they were rousted. A quick meal of bread, cheese, and what was left of the kid was consumed, and they were again on the way.

The flaps on the truck were left up now, and they could see the endless sea of sand all around them. In fact, it did look like the sea it once was, with the top of each dune the crest of a wave in mid-heave. But these sand waves were bigger than any of water, and they stretched as far as the eye could see.

Carter felt Ruth's warm breath at his ear. "It's eerie, isn't it?"

"Very," Carter whispered back.

"Wouldn't it be nice if we should run into a caravan or perhaps some desert bandits?"

Carter suppressed a laugh. "In this place we could pass

within a hundred yards, and all Bachman would have to do is cut the motor for a few minutes and they would never know we were here."

They had taken his watch, but by the moon Carter figured it was about three in the morning when they stopped. Again, Bachman appeared at the open flap.

"Everyone out, we're here!"

As they piled out of the truck, Bachman barked orders to each and every man, and each of them jumped to his tasks.

They were in the well of a huge wadi or valley between dunes that reached some seventy feet. Where they stood, the dunes had leveled off into a hard crusted plain of sand. At the open end of the wadi there were five wide-spreading thorn trees and a barren well. At one time the place had obviously been an oasis.

All around the well the ground was littered with dried pellets of camel dung. Skeletons of those same camels, still covered with hide and mummified in the dry, hot desert air, could be seen protruding from the sand.

Ruth and Carter were shackled to one of the thorn trees, and the men each took a gasoline-powered blower from the rear of the truck.

"What are they doing?" Ruth whispered.

"I would guess they are uncovering the airplane."

The words were scarcely out of his mouth when the roar of the blowers' little engines filled the wadi. The men, led by Bachman, started at the base of a huge dune and worked their way upward. In minutes they could see a Plexiglas bubble emerging from the sand.

"My God."

"Bachman was right," Carter growled. "He did have all this well planned."

Within a half hour they had the face of the bubble cleared, and through it they could see the outline of the Phantom fighter-bomber. The inside of the bubble itself was supported by wooden pillars and trapped air that had evidently been pumped in as the sand was scooped over the Plexiglas.

The more sand that was blown away, the more the Plexiglas began to sag. But before it sagged lower than the supporting pillars, Zayak Boudia had burrowed through the sand under the bubble and was climbing into the forward cockpit of the plane.

Bachman had his men trained well. Just as the two jet engines fired into life with an ear-shattering roar, the vents on the bubble were opened. As the air escaped, the now pliable bubble was rolled up. When the Plexiglas was high enough for clearance, Boudia taxied the plane out.

The tail had barely cleared when the bubble collapsed completely. While Boudia taxied the Phantom to the closed end of the wadi, the rest of the men were already at work with the blowers, filling in the sand over the collapsed plastic tent.

"Neat," Carter said, "very neat."

The jet and the blowers shut down. The moment they did, Bachman again started barking orders.

"We have two hours before dawn. You, shave Carter and get him into the overalls."

The Killmaster couldn't suppress a smile. Quickly he turned to Ruth. "This is all supposition, guesswork and hope, but it's all we've got. Listen up—"

"Hurry, they're coming this way!"

"Boudia will have to skim the sand all the way to the Red Sea while he's in flight to avoid radar detection. That will make his flying time almost double. If they want to strike at morning prayers—which I think they do—they'll have to take off just before dawn. That's to our advantage."

"It is?"

"Darkness, honey, even false dawn, would be great out

here for us. Starting right now, I want you to have to go to the toilet at least twice before takeoff.''

A little light went on in Ruth's eyes. ''The crewman with the droopy mustache?''

''Right. I saw the look in his eyes the last time he escorted you to the other side of the dune . . . pure lust.''

Her jaw clenched and a shiver went through her body. ''The son of a bitch wouldn't let me go out of sight. He wouldn't even turn around.''

''Be thankful that he won't. His hormones are probably going to save your skin. Bait him the first two times. The third time, just before we take off, you make the catch and reel him in.''

''I hope you know what you're doing. I'm not much of a seductress.''

''You just haven't looked at yourself the right way in a mirror lately.''

The two crewmen came up to them just as Carter finished speaking. One of them carried the small flight bag Boudia had taken the coveralls from earlier.

One of them said something to Carter in brittle, staccato Arabic. Carter's Arabic was good, but this man's dialect and regional accent lost him, so the Killmaster turned to Ruth for a translation.

''He wants you to lean back against the tree with your face in the moonlight.''

''Tell the bastard I can shave myself.''

Ruth reiterated, and got an angry, even faster reply.

''He says to do as you're told. They are afraid that you will kill yourself.''

''Fat chance of that,'' Carter said, scooting around in the sand.

The bearded crewman started taking utensils out of the bag. Ruth jumped into her part with the crewman with the droopy mustache. The man was actually smiling as he followed her toward the other side of the dune.

Carter shook his head in disgust as the man spit into a shaving mug and then used it to produce lather. He applied it liberally and then opened a plastic bag.

Now Carter was smiling through the lather.

The man was fitting an old-fashioned, single-edged blade into an old-fashioned, single-edged razor. Carelessly he dropped the paper wrapping from the blade to the sand. It lit right beside the dozen or so other blades that had spilled out from the plastic bag.

As the man started to shave him, Carter snaked his hand across the sand and palmed two of the blades.

FOURTEEN

It was false dawn, ghostly gray over the endless sand, when Boudia and Otto Bachman himself came to get Carter. Boudia carried the blue flight bag, Bachman a parachute over his shoulder.

They kept the leather thongs on his wrists as the two of them engineered him into the chute.

"I'm untying your hands now," Bachman said. "Please don't try any eleventh-hour heroics."

To give his words weight, one of the two armed crewmen moved in behind Carter, his machine pistol poised.

The Killmaster managed to keep a stone face as they took his Luger and Hugo, the stiletto, from the flight bag. As they rolled up his right sleeve, Carter could almost read the media phrase going through Bachman's mind: *An American agent, partially identified by the weapons he was known to always have on his person, was found in the burned wreckage of the Israeli plane . . . .*

The spring-activated chamois sheath was attached to Carter's right forearm. Then the Luger's rig was strapped to his right ankle. The gun itself went in last, after Bachman had shoved the empty clip into the butt.

167

For the first time since the entire affair had begun, Carter was glad of the German's thoroughness. He only hoped Bachman had slipped up on one small thing:—the single shell left in the chamber when Maruja Ortega had taken the clip out in the first place.

"Let's proceed!" Bachman barked.

"W-wait a second," Carter replied, holding back, hoping that his stuttering speech pattern sounded like fear.

"What is it?" the other man said impatiently.

"What happens to the woman?"

"Fräulein Melzer? Ah, I am afraid she must disappear," Bachman replied, almost relishing the words.

"Is that really necessary? When this is done, she can't really hurt you."

Bachman shrugged. "Forgive me, but thoroughness is one of my fortes. Let us go."

"Wait . . ." Again Carter hung back, dropping his eyes to the sand and digging in it with the toe of one boot. "Can I . . . well, say good bye to her?"

Bachman laughed. "Ah, sentimentality—even you have the weakness. Yes, go ahead, but hurry!"

Carter ambled to where Ruth was tied to the thorn tree. She lifted her face to his as he leaned forward, being careful not to touch anywhere except the lips.

Just before he kissed her, he spoke without moving his lips. "Can you do it?"

"Without a thought or qualm," she replied in the same manner.

They kissed, an open-mouthed, ardent kiss. And as they did, Carter flipped one of the wrapped razor blades from beneath his tongue into her mouth.

This done, he turned and walked rapidly back to the waiting group. "All right, you crazy bastard," he growled, "let's get this show on the road."

As Boudia and Bachman led him to the plane, with the crewmen trailing close behind, Carter glanced over his shoulder.

Ruth was already into her act, and her guard was only too happy to oblige.

Boudia went up one side of the plane at the rear cockpit, Carter up the other, with Bachman right behind him. They both helped him slide down into the narrow compartment. Then, and only then, did they remove the leather thongs from his wrists. They flattened his arms along the inside slide panels of the cockpit and then at the elbows, using the cross straps that would normally go across his chest.

As they worked they spoke, impervious to any reaction Carter might have.

"You are sure, Zayak, that this will secure him?"

"Positive," the Iranian sneered. "He cannot reach the instruments and he cannot escape."

"What if they find him tied like this, instead of strapped in?"

The pilot laughed. "The straps will be burned off, and probably his arms along with them. They will never know how he was strapped in, or why he didn't eject along with me."

"Good," Bachman said, placing the flight helmet on Carter's head and buckling the chin strap. "Should I fit the oxygen mask?"

"No need."

The German dropped to the ground. Boudia did the same on the other side and climbed into his own chute. When this was done, he climbed into the front cockpit and started strapping himself in.

Bachman gave him the thumbs-up sign and walked off toward the open end of the wadi, where the Azia brothers— Hadi and Omar—stood waiting. Both of the men held portable blowers in their hands. After the plane passed between them and into the sky, they would immediately start covering any traces that it had ever been in this part of the Sahara.

Carter glanced toward the thorn tree where Ruth had been tied. He could barely make out the leather thongs on the ground. She was nowhere in sight.

Good, Carter thought, everyone was accounted for.

He tensed his right arm. Just as he thought, they had broken the spring in the chamois sheath. There was no way to release the stiletto.

Then he lowered his left arm as much as possible and began shaking it.

It didn't take long for the razor blade to drop into his palm.

He was about three paces behind her. Keeping her hands close to her belly, Ruth removed the paper wrapper from the razor blade. She wadded it into a tiny ball and flipped it to light a few feet in front of her. When she reached it, she tramped it into the sand and twisted her foot to cover it.

She managed to get behind the second dune before he stopped her. "This is far enough!"

Before, her mind had been filled with anger, fear, frustration, and total embarrassment. Now she felt none of these things. She steeled herself to think of nothing.

Even though she had been in the field for many years, she had never been close to using the training she had received when she had first been recruited. She had never before been called upon to kill a man.

But she knew that, in this time and in this place, she could perform.

She had no doubt of it.

Instead of turning her body to the side and avoiding his leering eyes as she had in the past, Ruth turned and faced him full on as she unzipped her slacks.

Watching his eyes, she hooked her thumbs in the elastic of her underwear. Slowly she pushed them down, watching his reaction. Over her hips they went, and then down to her ankles. She paused a few seconds, letting his eyes get their fill before she squatted. When she did, she began unbuttoning her blouse and speaking at the same time.

"You're going to kill me, aren't you?"

"I do what I am told," he replied, watching her blouse open, the bulges of her full breasts rise with her breathing above the cups of her bra.

"I think the least you could do, as a man, is be honorable."

"How so?"

"Tell me the truth."

From her lowered eyes she saw him shrug and move forward until he stood over her.

"I understand that you must die, yes."

Suddenly Ruth reached down and pushed her slacks and panties off her left ankle. At the same time, she lay back in the sand, spreading her legs slightly.

"Then I have nothing to lose, do I?"

She passed her arm over her face as if to shield it from his eyes and her own eyes to the sun. As she did so, she dropped the razor blade into her mouth, positioning the blade outward between her teeth and settling her lips over it.

For almost a full minute, nothing happened.

She lowered her arm and looked at him.

Oh, my God, she thought, *no!*

He was standing, staring wide-eyed at her nearly naked body, his mouth hanging slack. He was paralyzed, seemingly struck into immobility.

Slowly, Ruth lifted her arms and parted them. She opened her palms and spread them.

It worked.

With a guttural growl, he dropped over her body, his hips shoving her thighs wide. His lips slobbered at her breasts as his hands tugged his robes up to his waist.

He was struggling with the drawstring on his trousers when Ruth curled her fingers in the thick hair on the back of his head.

As she tugged him up her body, she moaned and thrust her hips upward as if she were seeking him out. She felt his hot, bare flesh against her as he managed to kick his pants down.

She positioned her mouth two inches below his right ear and parted her lips, pulling them back from the blade. Then she pushed her tongue against the left half of the dull side so that it would protrude a little farther.

When she felt his hand wriggle between her legs, she tensed her arms, gripping his hair with all her strength.

Then she struck, twisting his head violently one way, bringing the blade between her teeth the other.

So fast did it happen that he made no sound.

But Ruth knew.

She felt the blood gushing from his throat pour over her face.

But she didn't stop there. She pulled his head back to her, this time her lips at his other ear. Again she slashed, cutting even deeper, and felt more blood flow.

She opened her eyes and blinked through the red haze. His head was up, pulled back so the flow of blood now spewed across her breasts. His effort to cry out made the blood pump even faster from the twin gashes in his severed throat.

Ruth spit the blade away and reached up with her hands. She clamped his jaw shut and squeezed his nostrils together until the attempted scream became a death rattle.

But still the eyes stared down at her, hating, and the body struggled.

"Die, die," she hissed aloud. "Die, you son of a whore who fucked a camel to breed you. Die!"

And at last he did.

Ruth heaved the body from her and used his robes to wipe away the blood, mainly from her face and eyes. She pulled on her underwear and slacks, and, not bothering to button her blouse, searched for and found the machine pistol he had been carrying, as well as two extra clips on his sash.

As she ran toward the dune that would hide her from the open mouth of the wadi, Ruth heard the jet's twin engines roar to life.

FIFTEEN

The engines roared in Carter's ears. From their pitch he knew they would be ready for takeoff in two minutes or less. Soon Boudia would lower the two canopies and lock them.

Once that was done, it was all over. If Carter tried to eject, he wouldn't have a prayer.

Inside the helmet sweat was streaming down his face, and he knew his clothing underneath the coveralls was soaked.

Using his left hand, he was three quarters through the strap holding his right arm. But it was tough going, very tough. The webbing was like cutting through hard leather for the thin blade. Twice his heart jumped into his throat when he thought the blade had broken. Another time he dropped it and, catching it, he had severely sliced his palm. Since then he had cut his arm in several places, trying to hack at the strap.

Every now and then he looked up to see that everyone was still in place. Bachman and the Azia brothers were still at the foot of the dune by the mouth of the wadi. The first guard was still out of sight with Ruth, and the bearded one

175

stood to Carter's right about fifty feet from the plane, his machine pistol slung carelessly over his shoulder.

"Just stay that way, buster," Carter hissed aloud.

There was only about a half inch left to cut through the strap now. He paused and jerked it with all his strength, but even that didn't work. The material was too strong. It wouldn't break and it wouldn't unravel.

With a curse he went back to work with the blade.

He saw movement in the front cockpit. Boudia had his arm in the air, one finger raised.

One minute.

Already he was swinging the tail around, lining up the nose with the open end of the wadi. Carter bit his lip, strained the material to the limit, and sawed as fast as he could.

It gave . . . and then came apart.

Instantly, Carter was a flurry of motion. He discarded the blade and quickly unsnapped his right arm. Then he ducked his head and pushed up the visor of the helmet for better vision.

The three-by-three red box was at his right knee. It was a double combination, one for the lid of the box itself and one for the plane's self-destruct mechanism inside.

Ignoring the heightened roar of the engines, he concentrated every bit of his mind on the rolling tumblers. There were six of them, and they had to each fall in sequence.

They did.

The lid popped, showing a tiny digital screen and a board of ten letter-number push buttons, much like a home telephone.

Again he concentrated: O-A-5-1-1-7-B-Z.

He pushed the buttons and saw the sequence come up on the screen. He eyeballed it one more time, and pushed the

"Fire" button until it stayed on.

Then he yanked the Luger from its ankle hoster and rolled, headfirst, out of the cockpit. The plane was already moving, and the canopy's hydraulics had started it in motion.

Carter had barely released his fingers when it closed and locked.

He landed on his feet in a dead run, leaning forward with the Luger in both hands before him.

The bearded crewman saw him, but wasted five seconds staring in open-mouthed disbelief.

Carter was only ten feet from him when the man finally swung the machine pistol smartly off his shoulder and brought it into play. He was a second too short of getting off even one burst.

Carter dropped to one knee, leveled, and fired.

The slug caught him dead center in the chest, sending him sprawling back into the sand like a stringless puppet. The Killmaster had already shoved the Luger into the side pocket of the coveralls and caught the other man's weapon in mid-flight when it left his hands. In the same movement, he whirled and ran in the heat wake of the plane.

He hadn't figured it all out, but the whole thing was falling into place better than he could have hoped for.

Boudia had swung the plane around far enough so the men at the end of the wadi hadn't seen Carter escape. Now the pilot was picking up speed in total ignorance that he had lost his passenger. And, better yet, the plane was still covering Carter's run.

With one hand he reached up, unsnapped the helmet, and threw it from his head. More air helped, but his lungs were still bursting. His legs and ankles were also taking a beating trying to run at sprint speed in the sand.

Then Boudia kicked his throttles to full. The heat was like

a furnace and the roar of the twin jets doubled. The plane leaped forward, its wheels barely kicking up sand as the jet approached takeoff speed.

Carter had already guessed the distance was impossible. Now he knew it, as the plane shot through the mouth of the wadi and on into the desert.

And three pair of eyes were staring in amazement at the running figure. The two Azia brothers dropped the blowers they had been holding and unslung machine pistols from their shoulders.

Carter was still a hundred yards away, but he had no choice. He started firing. He had little chance of hitting anything, and he didn't. But he was scaring the hell out of them.

Both brothers tried to get enough shelter behind the skinny trees to return fire. Bachman, his only weapon a Beretta, dropped close to the dune and started firing.

At that distance his handgun was about as effective as Carter spraying with the machine pistol at a dead run.

The Azia brothers were a different story. They were settled in and firing now. And they were quickly getting the range. Carter could hear the hiss of the slugs by his body and see sand being kicked up near his feet.

He moved his weapon toward them and kept firing in three- or four-slug bursts. He also kept running. He had no choice. He was going straight down the makeshift runway of the wadi, with no cover anywhere. The only other place he could go was up the side of a dune, and they would pick him off as if he had a target on his back.

Then he saw her, like a shimmering mirage on the wadi above and behind the brothers. With all the cool in the world, Ruth dropped to one knee and lifted the weapon.

She screamed once and then opened fire.

The range was about twenty yards, and she didn't let up

until the magazine was empty.

Only about half the slugs found their mark, but that was enough. She practically cut Omar and Hadi Azia in half.

Bachman suddenly realized what was happening and whirled to fire on her. But before he did, the world was rocked with a deafening explosion.

A mile to the south, they all saw a huge fireball rise into the sky, followed by ugly plumes of black smoke.

Bachman got the picture at once. He forgot Ruth and whirled back on Carter.

The two men were close now, not more than ten yards separating them. Carter brought up the machine pistol and fired. It clicked on empty and he didn't have another magazine.

Bachman laughed, cursed, and fired. Carter barely avoided the slug by diving facedown in the sand. The moment he lit, he started crawling forward, watching Bachman's eyes as he maneuvered for the next shot.

He wasn't going to make it, and he knew it.

Suddenly the side of Otto Bachman's head burst like an overripe tomato. Then the body was dancing across the sand, the legs somehow holding up the riddled, blood-spewing form before it fell.

Carter, still flat on the sand, looked up at the top of the dune just as Ruth sank to her butt.

She hadn't forgotten a spare magazine.

He couldn't move. He lay there for he didn't know how long. Nor did he care.

Finally, when his lungs were burning on what he felt was only a low flame and his legs had feeling, he used them.

But very slowly.

Step by step he went up the dune. Twice he had to rest before he reached the top. Then he was there, crawling his way toward Ruth who sat yoga style staring at his approaching figure but not seeing it.

"Jesus," he moaned when his eyes focused at last. "How bad are you hit?"

Her blouse was half ripped away. He could tell, barely, that she still wore her brassiere. It, like her whole upper body, her face, and her hair, was turning the dull brown color of dried blood.

At last he reached her and held her face in his hands.

"Ruth, how bad is it?"

"What?"

"The wound, where the hell are you hit?"

"I'm not," she said vacantly. "It's his blood . . . the razor blood. God, it was . . . it was . . ."

Then she was looking down at herself and she stopped speaking. Instead, she turned her head to the side and threw up, and kept throwing up.

Carter said nothing. He only held her head until nothing more would come. When that happened, he turned her into his arms and began rocking her.

"We did it, baby," he murmured in her ear, "we did it. That's all that matters. The plane's destroyed. That's all that matters."

They stayed like that for nearly an hour. Then she spoke, so low he could hardly hear her.

"What?" he asked softly, his lip near her ear.

"Get it off. Please, Nick, get it off of me!"

Suddenly he understood.

He got to his feet and tugged her up. Together, their arms around each other, they staggered down the dune on the outside of the wadi. Halfway to the truck, she started repeating it.

"Get it off, Nick . . . please, I feel like it's crawling on me. Get it off . . ."

"I will, baby, I will."

He found four jerry cans of extra gas and four of water

attached to the sides of the bed of the truck. They would need only two of the gas and one of the water to reach the Nile.

He took down three cans of water and carried them to the shaded side of the truck. In a bag in the back he found three more desert robes similar to the ones the crewmen had put on after they left the houseboat. One of these Carter tore into strips.

He stripped Ruth to her skin and threw her clothes to the side. Then he uncorked the three jerry cans of water.

"Hold your breath."

He emptied one can over her head and watched as it soaked her hair and ran down over her body. Then he had her lie down, and he washed her hair and her body with sand.

This done, he stood her up and dumped the second can of water over her.

"Better?"

"Yes, much."

"Almost through."

He soaked half the strips from the robe and scrubbed her thoroughly all over.

The third can of water was the final touch. It seemed to bring her back to reality. When he started to dry her with the remaining strips, she grabbed his hands.

"Thanks, but I can do it."

"The hell you can," he grinned. "This is the only relaxation I've had all day."

What he didn't get dry, the desert heat would. He got one of the two remaining robes and handed it to her.

"Get into this."

"What are you going to do?"

"Clean up this mess."

He carried two of the gas cans back to the wadi. When he had gathered the bodies into a single pile, he returned to the truck and stripped it of anything that would link it to Otto Bachman or his men.

Back in the wadi, he piled all these articles on top of the bodies, and scooped the sand around them to form a cauldron around the pyre.

When it was ready, he poured both cans of gasoline over the whole and lit it. The last thing he added was the set of Israeli flight coveralls from his own body.

As it burned, he gathered all the weapons and buried them.

After checking to make sure nothing would survive the fire except bones, he returned to the truck. When he had donned the last set of desert robes, he helped Ruth into the passenger seat and climbed into the driver's seat himself.

They had traveled almost fifty miles before she spoke.

"Where are we going?"

"The Nile, across from Kerma."

"Maruja?"

Carter nodded. "And Marcel Isban." He reached over and squeezed her hand. "You were sensational. But you're done. The rest of this scum is my problem."

SIXTEEN

Carter paced his driving so they would arrive at the Nile across from the small city of Kerma about dusk. Five miles from the Nile, at a small oasis, they ran into a small caravan heading in the same direction. It was another stroke of luck.

"How's your camel trading?"

"Why?" Ruth asked.

"I want you to barter this truck for two camels."

The *majib* of the caravan wasn't too happy about doing business with a woman, but he knew a good deal when he saw one.

Ruth was even less happy about riding a camel, but it was better than walking.

They arrived at the ferry crossing just after nightfall. Across the river, just a little downstream from the town, they could see the houseboat tied up to a private pier.

"There it is," Carter said.

"When will you go after them?"

"Right away," he replied. "They might be getting antsy with no uproar started about destruction in Mecca."

Across the river, they stabled the camels and found a

small café where they could watch the boat. Ruth ordered food as Carter scoured the riverfront for a paper. It wasn't easy to find, but he figured that was in their favor. If they got no news, then Isban and Ortega hadn't gotten any either.

They both wolfed down the food even though it was greasy and barely palatable. As they did, Ruth scanned the paper and Carter the boat.

He spotted the two crewmen, one fore and one aft. They sported no arms openly, but Carter was sure they both had some kind of weapon close at hand. From the way they alertly checked the city side and the desert across the river, it was obvious that they had orders to stay on their toes.

There was no sign of Marcel Isban or the woman.

"Nothing," Ruth said, folding the paper. "Not even a mention of an explosion in the desert. But this paper was printed last night."

Carter nodded. "They've got a radio on the houseboat, I'm sure, but Isban might be leery about using it until he's sure the strike is successful."

He got the stub of a pencil from the waiter, and wrote Mahmoud Bey's Cairo number on a paper napkin.

"Wait one hour and then call this number. Tell Bey what's happening. Also, tell him that, with any luck, there will be no trace of anything."

"You're going?"

"Yes."

"God, you're so damned confident."

Carter smiled. "Always, especially when surprise is on my side. When you see the lights come on in the wheelhouse, you can come aboard. It will be over."

Carter left the café and used small back streets to work his way upriver. When they had crossed on the ferry, he had spotted a series of storage sheds just on the edge of the town. Tied to the ramshackle piers in front of them were several small boats.

When he was up to the warehouses, he veered toward the river. In no time he was among them, moving through the pitch-black night to the water side.

There were four piers jutting out into the swiftly flowing Nile. All of them had small boats tied up. Carter chose the closest one and moved out to the end in a crouch. He slid down a slimy rope ladder and dropped into the nearest boat.

It was a little six-foot skiff with a single oar in the stern that also served as a rudder.

The Killmaster untied the skiff and immediately the current swept him from the pier.

The few lights of Kerma made hardly a dent in the darkness of the river. The moon was also too low to be a factor. Carter had taken the remaining three 9mm slugs from Otto Bachman's Beretta before he buried it. They were now in the clip of the Luger. The spring release was repaired on the stiletto sheath.

He was ready.

He kept close to the shore, so close that the bullrushes scraped against the little boat's hull. This was done for protection and to more easily control his speed.

The skiff seemed to be the only moving object on the vast expanse of the river. Occasionally the lights of a building or small house huddled between the river and the rim of the desert slid past. The gigantic dome of the star-strewn night seemed to be expanding into infinity. The craft seemed terribly tiny and impotent in the midst of the hush of darkness.

Carter could see the houseboat clearly now that he had passed the town of Kerma. Only a dim light gleamed on its bow, and another on the stern. She was built low in the water under a high superstructure, broken by glass doors and picture windows set in wide decks that were covered by scarlet awnings. In the low hull was a line of square windows.

Carter stopped the skiff and watched the two guards moving back and forth. He waited until the port deck facing the river was deserted, and then shoved off.

The remaining fifty yards was covered within seconds.

At such speed it was tricky keeping the prow on a steady line, but he managed. Then he was flying along amidships and at the stern. He grasped wildly for the stern anchor cable. He knew that if he missed, his chances of getting back upstream against the relentless river were slim to none.

His timing was perfect.

The skiff tried for a moment to get out from under him as he hung onto the cable. It was touch and go, but Carter managed to use his feet and guide it under the hull of the stern, out of sight from the deck above.

He waited, catching his breath, and listened. A minute, then two passed by before he heard the sound of footsteps. The guard checked downriver, and then moved away toward the wheelhouse.

Carter kicked the skiff away and watched it careen out of sight, carried spinning in the current until it was lost in the darkness. Then he crawled out the stern overhang and reached up until he could curl his fingers over the deck.

Seconds later he was topside and padding across the lounging deck to the stern of the wheelhouse. Up the ladder, he fell flat on his belly on the wheelhouse roof.

Already he could hear the footsteps returning. Tensing the muscle in his right forearm, he felt Hugo's warm hilt nestle into his right palm.

Just at the crewman came around the corner of the wheelhouse, Carter slid forward. In one movement he grasped the man's chin, yanked his head up and back, and struck with the stiletto.

The blow was true, in and up, through the pulpy part of the throat and into the brain.

There wasn't a sound, not even that of a falling body, as Carter slid forward and eased the body to the deck. He dropped down himself and dragged it to the stern. Very carefully, he eased the dead man over the stern by the ankles. When the body was submerged to the hips, he released it.

It disappeared as if by magic. Carter knew that the current flowed to the center of the river. And it was so powerful and swift and deep that the body could very well go all the way to Alexandria, and from there out into the Mediterranean Sea.

Carter moved forward, his ears attuned to any sound.

The second crewman was leaning over the bow, his elbows on the wood rail, a cigarette in his mouth. He was intently watching the stern lights of a launch going down-river.

The thrust was the same, and again there was no sound. As soon as the body was chasing the launch, Carter went below-decks.

There was a single passageway running fore to aft. There were six doors, three to a side. Light was seeping from beneath only one. Carter put his ear to it and heard the sound of a radio. It was tuned to a station playing Western music.

He smiled.

It was the same kind of mood music he had heard Maruja Ortega listening to in Bachman's guesthouse during his last visit.

At the same time, he heard the sound of a kettle whistle from the next deck down. That would be the galley.

Suddenly the whistle stopped, and the Killmaster knew he had them both positioned.

He retraced his steps to the deck and searched until he found a good-sized length of line. Back in the passageway, he tied one end of the line securely to the doorknob and the other to the handle of a locked case holding a fire extinguisher. The cabin door opened inward, but it would take the strength of ten men to open it now. And Maruja Ortega didn't have that kind of strength.

When the line was taut and secure, Carter headed for the ladder leading down to the galley. As he moved, he stowed Hugo and filled his hand with the Luger.

He didn't bother using the rungs of the ladder. He stepped on the top one and dropped down to the deck of the galley.

Marcel Isban was standing at a counter sipping from a cup. A Beretta was on the counter just a few inches from his right hand.

There was an instant of stunned silence, disbelief when their eyes met, and then Isban moved.

But he didn't move to the right, for the gun. He rolled left.

Too late, Carter understood why. He was diving for the light switch, and he made it. The room was plunged into darkness, and Carter hit the deck.

He fired once and then rolled away from the spot.

The Beretta exploded twice, the slugs slamming off the bulkhead where Carter had been standing.

Carter returned the fire with the Luger, aiming at the orange flashes from the Beretta.

There was a scream. Pots and pans and crockery clattered to the deck. Carter stood and took a few steps to his right, toward the light switch, and flanking Isban.

Carter knew that he had hit the man, but he didn't know how badly he was hurt. Also, Isban could still be hanging onto his gun.

He heard a groan, and there was another sound like feet

scraping along the floor. Then a soft, strangled voice, "I'm hit, damn you . . ."

The voice was strained, panicked. Carter knew the sound. He had heard the sound of dying men many times.

Isban groaned again. "Help me, I'm bleeding . . . help . . ."

Carter felt along the bulkhead until he found the light switch. He aimed the Luger at the sound on the deck, and flicked the switch. His finger was tightening on the trigger, but relaxed when the light came on.

Isban had lost the gun. He had gotten up onto his hands and knees, his head hanging down between his shoulders. He was wearing a white shirt, and there was a gaping hole in the back of it where the slug had exited. Around the hole was a spreading stain growing wider the more he moved. Beneath him, blood dripped from his chest to puddle on the deck.

Suddenly his legs and arms collapsed. He fell, his face striking the steel deck, his body sprawling, moving feebly. He looked like a crab scratching in the sand and not being able to reach the water.

Carter flipped him over onto his back with his toe, and knelt.

"Isban?"

The eyes opened, rolled, and then focused. "You . . . how . . . ?"

"I blew up Zayak and the plane."

"No . . ."

"Yes. Bachman's dead. And you know what, scum? You're dying."

"Hospital . . . doctor . . . please . . ."

"Remember Constance Graves, Isban?" Carter hissed.

"You, it was you . . . Slade . . ."

"Yeah, I killed Slade. Say hello to him in hell for me."

Carter left him to die and went back to the cabin deck. He untied the line from the doorknob and opened the door a crack, the Luger ready.

"Maruja?"

Silence.

"It's me, Carter. Come out."

More silence.

"It's over. Bachman is dead and Isban is down in the galley bleeding to death. If I have to come in there after you, I'm going to kill you."

"All right, I'm coming out."

The door opened and out she came, like a wildcat. In one hand she had a nail file, in the other a pair of scissors. Carter managed to avoid the nail file reaching his eye, but she got a good hit on his gun hand with the scissors.

The Luger fell to the deck and she went for it. Carter managed to kick it into the cabin. As it skittered across the floor, she went right after it, kicking the door shut in Carter's face.

By the time he got it open, she was by the bed coming up with the gun. He dived just as she fired, wildly. The last slug in the gun screamed through the door into the passageway. The Luger clicked on empty.

As Carter came up off the deck, his shoulder in her belly, Maruja slammed the butt of the Luger down across the back of his head.

She fell across the bed as he came down on her, hard. Screaming, biting, scratching, and still trying to brain him with the Luger, she twisted from beneath him. Half on and half off the bed, she struggled to her feet.

"Kill you, damn you, I'll kill you!" she shrieked, her eyes flashing, her naked body in a torn negligee gleaming with perspiration.

"Not if I kill you first."

He reached out, got a handful of the negligee, and yanked. There was a ripping sound as the garment tore loose.

She lost her balance. Carter's hands clutched her thighs and he pulled with all his strength. She came toppling back onto the bed. She fought now like an animal, her breath hissing from her in terror. Her fingernails slashed down across his cheek, dug in, held, ripped the flesh away. He managed to get her arms in a tight grip and rolled over on top of her.

Again she swung the Luger. Carter blocked the blow with a forearm and chopped it out of her hand. He pushed himself up on his knees, straddled her, and shifted his hands purposefully to her throat.

"Do you want to die, Maruja?"

In answer, she spit in his face and again tried to reach his eyes with her nails. Her legs and arms flailed out desperately.

Her eyes were wild. She had lost all reason.

Black insanity reached Carter for a moment, but he managed to hold it in check.

"I'm taking you back to Cairo, Maruja. Hopefully, they'll hang you."

Suddenly she stopped fighting. She lay there very still, eyes wide with resignation, looking up at him.

Carter relaxed his grip.

"No."

"No what?"

"Kill me."

Carter looked down at her. Her eyes were dull now, devoid of any spark of life. She was defeated, beaten. "Why did you get involved in all this?"

"I have always been in this," she murmured, her voice a dull monotone. "Why? Because I liked it. I liked the power of life and death. I enjoyed it, reveled in it. Bachman was a fool. He was a pawn for Marcel and myself. It was the two of us all the time. Otto was an idealist, but his money helped us achieve our goals. It helped us kill.''

Carter rolled from the bed in disgust. He returned to the galley and got Isban's gun. He emptied the clip and left one shell in the chamber.

Then he went back to Maruja's cabin. Inside, he threw the gun on the bed.

''There's one shell in the chamber.''

In the passageway, he retied the door and went up to the wheelhouse. He turned on all the lights and lit a cigarette.

He knew a spot. It was on the southern tip of Lake Nassar, one of the deepest lakes in the world. He would sail the houseboat there and sink her.

Then he saw the white-robed figure emerge from the darkness. Ruth was just stepping onto the gangway when they both heard the shot from below.

Ruth stopped, clutching the rail, her eyes wide as she looked up at him.

''It's all right. Come aboard,'' Carter said. ''It's over now. All over.''

DON'T MISS THE NEXT NEW
NICK CARTER SPY THRILLER

DEATHSTRIKE

Cautiously, Carter eased the barrel of the Mannlichter over the ridge of sand and fitted his eye to the Startron. Facial features became clear as he moved the scope from figure to figure.

One of the three figures at the fire was the woman. The man smoking at the palms was Abu El Adwan.

Carter eased the arms of the tripod forward and settled the bases into the sand. He locked a cartridge in and thumbed the safety to "off." Slowly he turned the focus ring until a dark spot was clear in the center of Adwan's chest. A quick adjustment of the windage and elevation screws, and he was set.

It took all of Carter's willpower not to take the man out then and there. But it would have been foolhardy and he knew it.

If the other four were El Adwan's backup—and now it was pretty obvious that they were—Carter would be a sitting duck on the dune all by himself. This was especially true since the Mannlichter was only single-action. The moment he fired, the other four would fan out and flank him before he could get off another shot.

He needed Ami and the firepower of the two Ingrams as his own backup.

Reluctantly, he eased the stock of the rifle to the sand and belly-crawled backward down the dune. Halfway, he lurched to his feet and jogged to the bottom.

In hushed tones he explained the situation.

Ami nodded his understanding and spoke with a new grimness in his voice. "The rendezvous was planned. They are with him."

"I'm afraid so," Carter agreed, "and I'm not surprised. He takes no chances with his own skin."

Hurriedly, Carter gave Ravelle a thirty-second lesson on firing and reloading the Ingram.

"Ami will take my right flank there, and you'll take my left, about seventy-five yards away. All you have to do is spray the area around the campfire. With this thing, you'll hit something. Just remember to keep the barrel down or the gun is liable to dance around and catch Ami or myself. Can you do it?"

She nodded a bit tentatively but gave Carter a little more confidence with the reappearance of the defiant, jutting jaw he now recognized so well.

"Good girl. All right, let's go . . . quietly."

But suddenly there was no such thing as quiet. A humming

sound arrested their movement. It quickly became a roar that filled the night. The three of them turned as one.

"There, to the south!" Ami hissed.

"Christ, a chopper!"

Even as Carter stared, the four-seater Bell, its whirling rotors gleaming in the moonlight, rose above the dunes and bore down on them. The machine loomed larger and larger, and suddenly twin landing spots flicked on from just above the sled.

Two hundred yards in front of them, the desert was turned from night into day.

"Quick!" Carter barked. "Spread, flatten out, and cover up completely!"

Ami and Ravelle lurched to the side as Carter dived for the lowest part of the gulley between the two dunes. All three of them went slithering under their robes like insects under rocks.

The Killmaster took quiet, even breaths, not moving a muscle as the sound of the chopper passed directly over him. He took his cue from the dark, the light, and the dark again, as well as the throbbing drone of the chopper's engine as it landed.

"Now!" he cried, bounding to his feet. "Up the dune!"

Carter was the first to the top. Quickly he surveyed the scene, now completely illuminated by the splashing light from beneath the chopper.

The engine was on idle, the rotors turning lazily. The pilot was still at the controls. A passenger—short, balding, in a dark suit and carrying a briefcase—had dropped to the ground. Just as he did, he slipped in the sand and fell to one knee, the light bathing his face and shoulders.

Carter heard a gasp from Ravelle a few feet to his left, but he kept his eyes on the tableau.

The small man moved toward El Adwan, who stood in the center of the other robed figures. There was little doubt now as to who the woman and three other men of the caravan actually were.

Each of them had produced Russian AK-47 rifles from beneath their desert robes.

Carter moved the Mannlicher around to focus on El Adwan. He adjusted the scope and squinted. Even though the man was stationary, he was constantly shielded by the restless guards.

The chopper's passenger reached him and they shook hands. They exchanged a few words and nods.

Carter sweated and waited.

Then they moved farther away from the chopper and into the darkness until there was just the two of them. But El Adwan walked on the far side, with the small balding man between himself and Carter with the sniper rifle.

The Killmaster readjusted the focus and range. It was about two hundred and fifty yards, with very little wind.

An easy shot.

A sure kill shot.

If the two men would only change places.

The minutes dragged on. The pilot in the chopper looked bored. Two of the guards dropped into a crouch and lit cigarettes. The woman wandered over to the chopper and exchanged a few words with the pilot.

Carter sweated some more, the tension building to a knot in his chest. With one finger he cleared the perspiration from his forehead and quickly returned it to the trigger. On either side of him he swore that he could hear Ami and Ravelle breathing.

Suddenly the balding man dropped to one knee. He set the briefcase on the ground and opened it. A tiny bulb came on, evidently powered by a battery within the case.

Furiously, Carter sighted in: focus right, elevation right, windage set, range . . . .

But before he could fire, El Adwan also went down, to his butt, so his entire body was once again obscured by the other man.

Carter cursed under his breath and tried to focus on the terrorist's bobbing head.

It was no good.

He chanced a quick glance at his watch, shielding the luminous dial with his hand.

The helicopter had been on the ground for twenty minutes.

He swiveled his eyes to Ravelle. She was game, the Ingram cradled in front of her, ready. She appeared calm.

To Carter's right, Ami appeared to be dozing, but the Killmaster could tell the truth of it when now and then he saw the muzzle swerve around to cover one of the moving guards.

El Adwan was up, shoving a package into his clothing. But so was the other man.

They started moving back toward the chopper, the terrorist still blocked by his companion.

Carter moved the muzzle of the rifle ahead of them. He was guessing. At the chopper, they would shake hands again. Then the balding man would climb in. For just that second, when the man was getting seated, El Adwan would be completely exposed.

For the last time, Carter adjusted the scope.

They reached the door. Just as Carter guessed, they shook hands. A few more words were exchanged, and the small man set his briefcase on the floorboards in front of the seat. He grasped the hand pull, put his right foot on the step, and pulled himself up.

Carter took a deep breath, eased it out, and fired.

"Damn!" Carter growled aloud.

The man's foot had slipped on the step, throwing him backward. In that instant, El Adwan had stepped forward to balance him.

It was just far enough.

The balding man had taken the heavy-caliber slug from the Mannlichter, and the loud crack of the rifle had resounded over the gentle idle of the chopper's engine. They were all alerted and they swung immediately into action.

Two of the four guards dropped to one knee and sprayed the ridge in Carter's direction with their rifles. The other two, one of them the woman, raced to the flanks, firing on the run.

The Ingram in Ami's hand was bucking, firing at the running figure on his side. But missing.

There was silence from Carter's left. The woman was frozen.

"Fire, Ravelle, dammit! Fire at anything!" Carter shouted, jamming another cartridge into the sniper rifle.

El Adwan had been galvanized into action himself, but not defensive. As usual, his first thought was himself.

He had wrenched the dead man around in front of him. Then, using the other man's body as a shield, he was now crawling into the chopper. Carter could see him barking orders at the pilot, and he knew exactly what those orders were.

The engine was roaring now and the rotors were picking up speed.

Carter sighted in on the pilot's head. It was a tough shot, almost impossible. The slugs from the two kneeling guards were kicking up sand all around Carter's head and the chopper was moving, lifting off the desert floor.

Wisely, the pilot was jiggling the machine from side to side as he got lift. El Adwan had brought his own rifle into play and was firing at the orange spurts that Ami's Ingram made in the night.

Then Carter got some peace and quiet. Ami had zeroed in on the two squatting guards. With a fanning burst he had raked them, sending them both flying backward to land, very dead, spread-eagled in the sand.

It was the lull the Killmaster needed. He sighted in. The chopper was about twenty-five feet off the ground and rolling its tail around. When the spin was completed, the silhouette of the pilot was dead center in Carter's sights.

He fired, and through the scope saw the pilot's head explode, the remnants spraying the far side of the Plexiglas bubble.

It was a perfect hit, but the Killmaster had other problems. The female guard, realizing that she was drawing no fire, had made a right angle and charged up the dune. Carter's shot drew her and she turned his way.

Suddenly she was charging over the rim, the bucking AK-47 in her hand on full auto.

Carter managed to roll away from the first burst as he struggled to get another cartridge into the Mannlichter.

Even as he jammed the bolt home, he knew he would be too late. The woman had spotted him and read the situation. She skidded to a halt and brought the muzzle of the gun around in a slowly deliberate motion.

At the last second, just before she fired, her eyes went wide and the rifle dropped from her hands. Carter heard the chatter of Ravelle's Ingram just as the woman's body lifted into the air and fell, lifeless, at his side.

He looked up. Ravelle knelt only two feet behind where the woman had been, her face stark white, the Ingram still, shaking in her hands.

"I'm sorry," she gasped.

"Better late than never," Carter said, leaping toward her.

He grabbed the Ingram and a magazine from the belt around her chest. In one movement he had reloaded and turned.

The chopper was still rising, slowly spinning in circles. He raised the Ingram and fired.

Halfway through the clip, he saw the hatch open. A body came through it and hurtled down to hit the sand. In the same instant, the chopper righted. The nose bent, the tail lifted, and it moved off.

Carter finished the magazine, but it was too late. In seconds the machine was over a dune and lifting into the night sky.

"You son of a bitch!" Carter screamed, watching it disappear.

El Adwan had kicked out the pilot's body and taken the controls himself.

—From DEATHSTRIKE
A New Nick Carter Spy Thriller
From Jove in April 1988